NO FIRE WITHOUT SMOKE

Danny Roden's Travelling Medicine and Jamboree Show pulls into Bradbury, hoping for a peaceful trip. But trouble quickly finds them in the shape of Jack Donovan. After a failed robbery attempt, Donovan disrupts the lady sharpshooter Smoke Winters' act. The bullets are soon flying . . . and the targets are all human. Before sunset, leaving a trail of blood in their wake, Donovan and his men flee town after kidnapping a small girl. With no one prepared to go after them, the task is left to Smoke Winters . . .

Books by Mark P. Lynch
in the Linford Western Library:

HOUR OF THE BLACK WOLF

MARK P. LYNCH

---◆---

NO FIRE WITHOUT SMOKE

Complete and Unabridged

LINFORD
Leicester

First published in Great Britain in 2016 by
Robert Hale
an imprint of The Crowood Press
Wiltshire

First Linford Edition
published 2019
by arrangement with
The Crowood Press
Wiltshire

A catalogue record for this book is available
from the British Library.

ISBN 978–1–4448–3980–7

Published by
F. A. Thorpe (Publishing)
Anstey, Leicestershire

Set by Words & Graphics Ltd.
Anstey, Leicestershire
Printed and bound in Great Britain by
T. J. International Ltd., Padstow, Cornwall

This book is printed on acid-free paper

1

This is the story of the lady sharp-shooter Smoke Winters, and how she went to Inferno, fought and died there, and then went back and fought all over again to save a child that was no blood relation to her and who held her to no promise that I ever knew about.

It ain't a ghost story, and it ain't nothing to do with resurrection either, at least not as it's written about in the Bible. It's not even about revenge. Or not in the way you might think.

The reasons Smoke did what she did . . . well, I guess they're complicated, and you'll have to work them out for yourself in the end. I have my own ideas, but the truth is that I can only tell you *what* she did and just a little bit about *why* she did it.

Settle in and give me some of your time. This is what happened.

★ ★ ★

Danny Roden's Travelling Medicine
and Jamboree Show rolled into Bradbury with little fanfare on the second
Monday in the month of May, 187 —.
Bradbury itself was a growing town in
those days. Unlike its nearest neigh-
bour, Inferno, from the get-go it had
about it a wise mayor and a group of
relatively honest selectmen with achiev-
able ambitions. As a result of careful
planning and wise investments — and
some would say not a little luck
— Bradbury had prospered over the
years while Inferno faded and died.

Bradbury now had a bank that did a
tidy business, and there was a station
that would see two or three stages a
day; there was more than just your
mercantile store, an undertaker's, and a
barber's on Main Street. Boutique
stores had opened, selling fine ladies
dresses and silk scarves among the
more traditional work-a-day clothes;
the painted writing on the windows of

the pottery store allowed that you could buy 'The best Chiner this side of the Ocean'; and there was in fact a genuine Chinerman who sold tea out of a big urn at the corner of Main and First, just a coupl'a bits for a tin mug full, which he'd wipe clean with a rag between customers.

Talk had been going on about setting up a district law court in town, and if things really did come to pass as planned, then a railroad sometime in the future didn't seem too unlikely a prospect either.

Bradbury was a happy, leafy place. It was prosperous. Its citizens, which numbered toward the nine hundred mark, walked the boardwalks and shot the breeze with one another. Dogs ran freely but none of them were dangerous. Of the three saloons there was only one where a decent man was wise to keep his head down and leave after just one drink. (So yes, there was darkness here, but it was thought to be a small affordable darkness.) Children played

3

kick-the-weasel on lawns in front of wooden houses that sprang up like mushrooms, and they attended the school that Matt Rusby and his wife ran on Mondays, Wednesdays and Fridays, from ten in the morning until three in the afternoon, with an hour's rest for lunch and prayers.

It was just the sort of place that Danny Roden's Travelling Medicine and Jamboree Show should be able to come, pin up a few posters, hand out flyers, and expect to do good business before moving onto the next town on its wayward itinerary across the West. Maybe, in the course of its stay, a few hearts would be broken, but that was just the way it went, like a summer breeze.

Danny usually sent word ahead that the show was coming, make as much of a procession out of it as he could manage. 'Publicity's the key,' he'd tell anyone who would listen. I know he told me enough times I was able to chorus the phrase right along with him.

He liked to ride into town high on the buck seat of the lead wagon, wearing his best glittery showman's suit, a hollering and a whoopin' and calling out how we'd arrived, here was Daniel J. Roden's Travelling Medicine and Jamboree Show, come and see the show, folks, come and see the show.

He'd wave his hat and give everybody the biggest smile he possessed as he hollered out, tip a lady a wink if he thought he could get away with it too.

But it had been a hard slog to Bradbury and we were all tired. We'd been struck by a run of bad luck of late. We hadn't made much money during the last two stops, we'd narrowly missed being struck by a thunderbolt, had to hide out from Indians, and a wheel had come uncoupled from the medicine wagon during a heavy downpour, meaning a lot of time hastening on repairs in the darndest weather. We were tired and glum, and all a little wanting in the belly.

Danny hadn't, on this occasion, sent

anyone ahead to pave the way. The horses hadn't been brushed down and decorated, the dried mud chipped off the wagon wheels; and it was with only a half-hearted flourish that the five wagons that comprised our little troupe had been uncovered so you could see the merchandise and turns — as the acts were known — inside.

You'll appreciate, then, that it was a weary looking show that entered Bradbury, raising barely a cry to advertise its wares, the medicine stall and the entertainment we'd eventually provide in a field on the outskirts of town.

★   ★   ★

Although we didn't make a fuss of our arrival, a couple of younger folks hit up and followed us through to the rough circle we made on the spare scrubland not so far from the livery.

Danny had handed out a few sweet-tasting candies to the kids who'd run after us, and told them to come on over to the show, bring their parents when it was up and running. But his smile was tired, his salesman's patter running on automatic. When we hauled up, he set me to getting the entrance ready. And though I'd objected many times that anyone could walk in any which way they pleased — the entrance was, after all, only a couple of tall fence posts I was putting up with some bunting strung around them; there was no surrounding barrier — Danny still had me go about it.

'It's for appearance's sake, Luther. So much about this business is appearance. It's showmanship.'

I knew there was no use in arguing; I went around to Clete's wagon and asked for the posts. Clete was a big, ageing black man who looked after the horses and general wellbeing of the wagons. There wasn't a strut or plank he didn't know how to plane and fix if called upon to do so. I'd even seen him pound up an improvised shoe to put on a horse one time. If it hadn't been for

Clete, we'd be a wagon or two short of a train right now.

'Boss got you hammering these things again?' he said with a smile.

'Yes, sir. Though I don't see the point.'

'Ain't a whole lot in this world that makes a point, Luther. You'll learn that one day. And if you a wise boy you'll come to accept it.'

I took the posts, which I saw Clete hadn't sharpened up since I hammered them into the ground at our last stop, and the spade and big lump hammer, staggering a little with the weight. I was only young, and it seemed like I was being put to hard labour for no real point.

It took a lot of time; I stripped down to my bare chest because I'd raised a good old sweat and didn't want to stink up my shirt. I was pounding on the second post, having dug a decent sized hole for it and climbed the swing-ladder to get to the top, when I heard voices working up to an argument.

I skinned away some of the moisture on my forehead and squinted over to see what was going on.

Danny was standing with three rough-looking guys, maybe cowboys, maybe gunhands. All of them were taller than him, all were pretty unkempt, with a lot of facial hair and a mean vindictiveness to their airs. For some reason, no one was about to see them but me, leaving Danny facing up to the men alone.

Now, Danny was in his mid-thirties at this point, and while he was nobody's fool, he wasn't a gunhand. He'd boxed in his younger days, and the rumour went he could still throw a punch, but if he didn't strike one of these big men and that man go down with that punch, then he was in trouble. He knew it too, and was trying to argue his way out of the situation.

'Now, gentlemen,' Danny was saying. 'Ain't no need for this kind of talk. We come here without wishing to make anyone's trouble. We're just a peaceful set, looking to entertain, sell some medicine and lucky charms.'

'But you see,' the elder of the three said, 'me, Joad, and Spike here, we've come a long way. Haven't been in town too long. But we've run across your kind before. Spike don't talk much, it's on account that he lost his voice some months back, after trusting to some medicine off of a wagon looked very much like yours.'

Danny shook his head. 'Wasn't my band's wagon, sir, I can promise you that.'

'They're one and the same to us, mister. I got so I don't hold any faith with you and your kind now.' The man tilted back his hat, revealing a tan line on his rough forehead. 'Perhaps to compensate us for the misfortune your fellow medicine show dispensed upon Spike here, you could hand over a few dollars. We was thinking maybe fifty — that right, Spike?'

'Fifty dollars?' Danny said.

'Don't seem an awful lot to compensate a man for losing the ability to talk, but it's a beginning, and we're not greedy people. Don't ever let that be said of us.'

I looked around to see if there was any help, but after a busy hive of activity the scrubland behind the livery was deserted. A lot of the show folk would be in town now. Buck Wheeler and Wheat Rayne would be in a saloon, or else, knowing Buck, whoring already, while the others would be putting up posters and passing out flyers. Clete wasn't in his wagon when I glanced over there, and the only person I could see was Cara Treene. She was older than Danny and wider than Clete, and for all the second sight she claimed to possess didn't seem aware of anything untoward going on right now.

If anyone was going to back Danny up, then it would have to be me. I came down the ladder and moved on over, trying not to quiver as I shucked on my shirt. All I'd got to help me out was the big old lump hammer, which I didn't think would hold up too well against whatever handguns those guys had. Danny was trying to be reasonable. The one called Spike looked at me and shook his head with no obvious show of emotion. All three of them had faces like reptiles. Their eyes were dead. I could feel myself losing the grip on the hammer even as I stood beside Danny.

'Gentlemen,' Danny said, 'now what you're asking don't seem a fair proposal to me. Why, you'd no sooner expect a smithy to make reparations to you for work some other smithy did, now would you?'

''Tain't a matter of some other guy. More I look at your wagon there, the one with the fancy writing on it,' their leader said, 'more I think that's the same truck sold Spike that medicine made his voice disappear.'

Spike nodded slowly. It was a bit like watching a rock move. The other one, fat Joad, spoke now, upon being asked to confirm his friend's suspicions. 'Rightly so, I reckon.'

His voice was high and hoarse, as if

his throat had been cut in the past. Whatever medicine Spike had taken, it sounded like he'd shared it with his compadre here.

'That's the same wagon all right, Jack.'

'Which means,' the one called Jack said, 'that by my reckoning, you're the one cost my pard here the use of his voice, mister. Now I think on it, that should be worth a lot more in compensation than a measly fifty bucks. Spike don't know he'll ever be able to talk again, and that money wouldn't last him out his life.'

Danny said tightly, 'You know we didn't sell you any medicine. You're trying to rob us.'

'That a fact?'

'Yes, sir. I think it is.' Danny was locked in a staring contest with Jack. He said to me without breaking his gaze, 'Luther, you hear this man, understand what he's doing?'

'Yes, sir, Danny. I hear him.'

'This man is trying to take from us

what rightfully ain't his to take. He thinks he's seen an opportunity. He's come along into this town — by the looks of him and his buddies, they've been travelling and aren't settled here with regular work — and he's seen us, thinks we're an easy target.'

None of the men spoke.

Danny said, 'Here I am, all alone except for a 16-year-old boy by my side, so there must be a way of taking money off the guy. That's what these gentlemen are thinking. Now I don't know if Spike here has lost his voice or not — he surely ain't said nothing so far, that's the truth — but it don't make a whit of difference. We ain't responsible for what happened to him and we won't be paying any kind of compensation they're after.'

Jack spoke so low I almost missed what he said. 'You really think this is a wise way to behave in front of the boy?'

'Boy's near enough a man now.'

'Way I see it, you're unarmed and he's shaking in his boots, hands so

14

slippery he can hardly hold onto that hammer.'

'That may be true. But it's also true that I ain't gonna volunteer any money to you. You want it, you got to take it off us. That'd make it robbery. And although we ain't been here long, I noticed there was a sheriff's office on Main Street and that a couple of deputies were walking around with stars on their vests. This ain't a lawless town.'

Jack chewed on his cheek and nodded. He tugged his hat forward.

'And you think I don't know any of that?' he said.

'Just wanted to remind you,' Danny said.

'Hey, Jack.' Joad pulled on Jack's left arm. He did that, it meant Jack's right hand was still free to draw his iron if he'd a mind to. 'We got company on its way.'

Jack finally broke the stare he was putting on Danny and pinched a look over his shoulder. I dared let my breath out when I saw what Joad had seen. Coming toward us, and surely the most welcome sight I could have asked for, was a tall figure wearing a silver badge and a side-shooter.

'I think you should count this your lucky day,' Jack said to Danny. 'Very lucky indeed.'

With that, as the sheriff came toward us, the three men started slinking away like shadows around the back of the wagons.

'Luther, I don't want the sheriff moving us out to save on trouble. Make like nothing's happened here,' Danny said low enough that the sheriff couldn't hear. 'Go keep an eye on those guys, make sure they leave without touching anything.'

As I went to do that Danny put on his hale and hearty showman's voice. 'Well, Sheriff, mighty good of you to come out here and say hello.'

'Name's Winn Sommers,' I heard the sheriff say as I ran off. 'The law in these parts. Good to have you all here.'

The gunmen went around the side of the livery and into town. Although Danny hadn't said to go after them once they'd left our camp, I followed all the same. They were bad men, I understood that, and most of the folks in town knew it too. As they walked down the street, empty spaces opened up on the boardwalks for them, and conversations fell into silence as they passed. Danny had read them right: they were dangerous.

I watched from across the street and a ways back behind them, keeping people in between us when I could. If they knew I was spying on them then they didn't let it show. I did my best to be cautious. I hoped that was enough.

They got to the end of Main, where it began to peter out into store- and grain-houses, leaning buildings and shacks sinking into disrepair. There was a crummy looking saloon with only one of its batwing doors intact, and even that one was hanging at an angle so that it clanged the door-frame when you pushed through it. The other was propped up against the side of the front wall, beneath a set of windows that were half boarded up. The place smelled of sour beer and stale tobacco even from where I was standing.

Deciding I'd gone far enough in pursuit — the men could be in there all day — I turned around to head back, when I saw a Daniel J. Roden's Travelling Medicine And Jamboree Show poster trodden into the ground.

I picked it up, dusted it off. But without any pins to put it on a wall, the best I could do was slide it into a window-frame as I walked down Main Street towards First and the right turn that led out to the scrub where Danny had us setting up.

2

The first time I saw Smoke Winters, she was dressed in beige trousers and a cotton blouse, her white hair loose and shining in the sun. She was setting up a line of pine-cones on the trunk of a fallen tree, evenly spaced about a foot apart.

It took me a moment to realize she was going to try to shoot them.

I was fourteen years old; she was in her early twenties and I thought she was about the most beautiful thing I'd ever seen. I didn't know that I believed in angels, but if I had, then she ought surely to be one. My heart swelled so much at the sight of her that it felt like I didn't have room enough left in my chest to breathe.

She saw me standing there — I guess I was a picture, open-mouthed and awkward — and she smiled and sashayed toward me, thumbing shells into her pistol. She didn't wear a hat and her hair was so bright above her fair face that it made her look like she'd come from the moon.

'I charge for watching,' she said easily enough. 'You're the new boy, aren't you? Danny told me he'd hired someone on. You know, it's not polite to spy on a person, 'specially not a woman. What's your name?'

'I wasn't spying or nothing, honest. I was just — '

'So what's your name?' She clicked the cylinder in place and gave it a spin. With a thumb on the hammer, she rested the gun against her chest as she waited for me to speak.

'Luther, miss.'

'Anything else come with that, Luther?'

I shook my head confused.

'A last name,' she explained.

'Oh. Yes, ma'am. Connolly. Luther Jay Connolly.'

'Pleased to meet you, Luther Jay Connolly.'

'Ma'am. Likewise.'

She smiled and turned away from me, holstered her pistol. I suppose it was wrong to admire her from behind, but I couldn't help it. She was a fine woman.

'Stop calling me 'ma'am',' she said over her shoulder. 'Folks call me Smoke. That includes you from now on, you hear?'

'Yes, ma- . . . yes, Smoke. And it's good to meet you too.'

I wondered if I should say something else, though I wasn't sure what that something else should be. As it was, I didn't have a chance to form a word before she put her pistol to use.

In about the time it'd take me to blink, she drew her gun and the pine-cones she'd lined up shattered into pieces one after the other. Along with the echo of the shots, gunsmoke and the smell of cordite hung in the air. Smoke Winters turned and blew across the muzzle of her pistol and passed on by me, swinging her hips and dropping me a wink as she went, leaving me looking at the destruction she'd so casually wrought.

'Just keeping my eye in,' she said and then she was gone.

★ ★ ★

It wasn't so much a question of me signing on with Danny's Travelling Medicine and Jamboree Show as it was Danny taking me under his wing and deciding to do the right thing by me. Danny was from Irish stock, like my own pa was, and when Ma and Pa had their cart accident, the show just happened to be in town. Freshly orphaned, with not even the tar-roofed shack I grew up in to my name, or Horace the lame mule that used to pull Pa's wagon, Danny heard about this and took me in.

They say that bad things happen to good people for reasons we don't understand, that it's the Lord's hand in these matters. But I sometimes wonder if it ain't true and that the Devil plays his part as well. I know when we buried Ma and Pa — they went in the same small plot my sister Stephanie occupied in the town cemetery, under a wooden cross Pa himself had built for her when she died of river fever the year before — there was some that said they deserved their rest and were at peace now, could be happy that they'd got their daughter back, thank the Lord. Part of me wasn't so sure how kindly those words were, because it sort of meant Ma and Pa wouldn't miss me wherever they were now. But I understood the sentiment even if I didn't understand any plan God might have.

After the funeral, Joey Buckhannon, an old friend of Pa's who spent most of his time sitting drunk in the saloons, asked me what I planned on doing.

'I was thinking of maybe selling what holdings I got title to, putting the animals and Horace out to anyone who'll take them, and see about buying me an apprenticeship in town. Maybe at the smithy. I don't think farming's for me.'

But things didn't work the way I expected. I didn't understand that to make his claim on the land and set up the farm, little tar-roofed shack and all, Pa had borrowed money from the bank. I learned about this when Pa's last will and testament was read out. I suspected that something wasn't right when I saw there was a piggy-eyed fat man smoking on a big cigar in the room, as well as the narrow lawyer, who went by the name Rodderick, presiding over matters.

Turned out the fat man was Mr Turner from the local bank, and he was there to make sure he got out of Pa's estate what he saw was his. Turned out Pa had other creditors too, had run up debts at various stores in town. When all the legal beans had been moved from one counter to another, there wasn't nothing left for me. Not even old Horace the mule.

'You can leave now,' Rodderick told

me. 'There's nothing more needs to be done here. You can't go back to the farm, it ain't yours any longer, and everything there is someone else's property now.'

I was dumb with shock as I left. I didn't really notice the posters pinned up along the streets or pasted onto store windows, so it didn't register with me that Daniel J. Roden's Travelling Medicine and Jamboree Show was in town. I just put my feet to use and wandered around in a daze, not knowing where I should go or what I should do now I hadn't got a home.

I spent the next days around town. The show was there most of that week. I didn't go. I overheard how Ma and Pa's holdings had been divided up, the tar-roofed shack emptied out. I couldn't bear to go out and see. Pa's creditors had claimed the swine and chicken but I never did learn what happened to Horace. I lived on any scraps I could find, the kindness of folks, discarded food and dropped pennies. Even though I'd been reduced to a state of homelessness, I wasn't about to start pickpocketing or stealing. Pa wouldn't have allowed that.

Thin to start with, it wouldn't be long before I was trimmer than a hoeing rake.

On the third night, I was out sleeping rough, just after a thick rain had gone mean and turned into a deluge. I was huddled up between two barrels that caught rainwater off of the gutters of the mercantile store and protected me from the worst of a drenching. Some time toward midnight a man with the blackest skin I'd ever seen lurched out of the rain to find some shelter.

His name was Clete Lennox, and he was with Danny Roden's travelling show. He saw me and said, 'Now how come a fine white boy like you is out in the rain, wasting away so you could fall between the gaps in the boardwalk?'

A couple of days later I was riding with the wagons, leaving behind my hometown, and the small cemetery where Ma and Pa slept beside my sister. I was part of Daniel J. Roden's Travelling Medicine and Jamboree Show.

★   ★   ★

Two years on, I'd learned to speak to Smoke without drooling, though I sometimes felt a flush rising in my cheeks if she looked into my eyes for too long a time. She must have known how I felt around her, but you could count the times she teased me about it on the fingers of a one-handed man suffering from leprosy. Of course, that kindness only had me admire her all the more.

As we readied for the show in Bradbury, I had the job of putting up the targets for her to shoot. Although not many men would come out and say as much to one another, let alone to any wives or sweethearts they might have, Smoke Winters, Lady Sharpshooter, was the main reason they came to see the show more than once.

Danny called it showmanship, the outfit Smoke wore for her shooting act. I don't know what I'd call it, but it was always pleasing to see her in it. Smoke's hair had turned a premature white when she was young for reasons she never spoke about, or so I'd been told. To bring it out brighter, she used some of the unguents that went into the medicine show bottles, and set it off by wearing an outfit that Cara Treene sewed her into before each show.

The outfit was ice blue and had white tassels on the arms and around her legs, but the tassels weren't designed to distract from Smoke's nicely shaped body and I don't think any warm-blooded man had ever had to contend with that as an issue.

She wore a white hat with a wide brim that couldn't hide the youth and beauty of her face. Something else it didn't stop you seeing was the look of determination that shone in her eyes. If you weren't paying close enough attention, you could miss the flashes of darkness that sometimes surfaced in her expression. They were only fleeting. But they were there.

'You want the smaller targets today?' I asked her.

Depending on her mood, Smoke might stand closer to the targets than on other days, hold off on the trickier shots for days when she felt she couldn't miss a thing.

'Small as we've got,' she told me with a smile.

'Yes, ma'am!'

She laughed at that. Didn't scold me for not calling her Smoke either. We both knew I was getting a little too old for her to be scolding me.

This was our second show in Bradbury. The first one had gone off well, the gunmen hadn't come back, and a lot of the townsfolk had attended. We'd raised enough word of mouth for Danny to declare it worth staying for a second, third, and perhaps even a fourth day.

Clete had said to me after the first show, 'We sold an awful lot of that sugared honey medicine eases a person's throat today.'

I thought about the ugly gunhands, the one who did all the talking, Jack, saying how it was a medicine show product that had left his friend Spike without a voice. Well, sugar and honey medicine wouldn't cut a man's throat up to nothing, and we didn't sell anything dangerous. However Spike lost his voice, it wasn't through any medicine we were selling.

'That's good,' I said.

'Uh huh. Make up for the last few stops where we've not made the money we should have done.'

'People been tight with their purses of late, that's true, ain't it, Clete?'

'It is. But don't you go forgetting, we're on the edge of the civilized world here. Beyond Bradbury things get wilder. They still got Indian troubles to contend with, and a man has to watch out for hisself. Frontier land, it can bring out the best in a man, but it sure knows how to trouble you too. Worse than that, it can call to men who don't have the kind of consideration for each other that folks like you and me have. They an awful lot like wolves, these men, Luther.'

'You're talking about those who tried hitting up on Danny, aren't you?'

'Them or people like them. What Danny did was brave, facing them down. But if the sheriff hadn't arrived when he had . . . '

'You think he should've given them the money?'

'Live to fight another day. Sometimes you got to learn to do that, Luther. Much as your pride tells you to take your beating or risk getting shot.'

Clete was still a big man, despite his advancing years. When Thunders Gru, a wrestling champ in a rival jamboree show, had been making fun of our little troupe a season back, Clete had stepped into the ring with him and whupped him up but good. Clete'd taken hold of him by the neck, invited Thunders's nose to make acquaintance with his forehead, and then, when blood was oozing down Thunders' chin, had raised his knee swiftly and without anything holding him back into Thunders's gentleman's region.

The only thing Danny had said to Clete as they were carrying Thunders away was 'You should'a saved that for his show, Clete, then you could've taken the prize money.'

Clete had replied, 'I got prize enough out of this without needing to take his money off of him too.'

I said now, thinking on that wrestling match, 'But you never back down, Clete.'

He smiled, showing me his big teeth. 'What you about now anyway, boy?'

'Putting the targets up for Smoke.'

'Spending a lot of time with Smoke these days, ain'tcha?'

I shrugged.

'You getting up to seventeen soon. Might have to take you to a special lady

I know. She'll see about fixing you up so you don't have to go round walking funny all the time you're around Smoke,' he said and winked.

Not knowing what else I should do, I smiled and thanked him, then made my way back to where Smoke's shooting show was going to take place. I'd the targets she wanted in my arms. High above, the sun was brighter than a silver dollar. It looked like it would be a fair nice show.

3

His name was Jack Donovan and he was, by anyone's notion, a bad man. He'd been drinking heavily, along with his crew, Silent Spike and Joad Rogers. For a week now they'd pretty much owned the saloon. Even the local tough guys had learned to give them a wide berth and to speak to them respectfully.

To lay down his claim to the bar, Jack had emptied the contents of a bottle of rum over the head of the local rooster. Did it without opening the bottle too. Just took it off the barman, swung it an arc, and smashed it over the guy's head. Joad had said to Jack, as if nothing much worth commenting upon had happened, 'You not like the taste of that rum, Jack?'

Jack lit a cheroot he'd rolled and breathed out a plume of smoke. 'Not really my thing, rum.'

His match was still alight and he looked around it, down to where the rooster was on his hands and knees, groaning at the bloodied gash that parted his rum-drenched hair. The guy tried to say something, but the way I heard about it later, it just came out as a low moan. The rooster made the mistake of putting a hand on Jack's boot. He most probably was looking for help, and with his head leaking like that, the blood running in his eyes, wasn't caring where that help came from. But Jack's help was the kind of help a man shouldn't ever seek out.

Joad said, 'Need to cauterize the cut, that's what I heard from a friend of mine joined up with the cavalry and got wounded. A hot poker, that stops the blood coming out.'

'That right?' Jake said.

'Don't see no hot poker around here.'

'Guess he'll have to make do with whatever's to hand,' Jack said, and put his match to the tough guy's head.

Flames rose from the rum that had

soaked into the rooster's hair, quickly followed by the guy's anguished cry. Jack had to push him back, make sure he didn't singe his vest, a garment of which it turned out he was particularly fond.

'Whoa, there,' he said, trying not to laugh.

The rooster screamed, batting at his hair, and thrashed around the floor.

'Think that's enough fire to do the job?' Joad said.

'Better make sure, I guess. Wouldn't want him to bleed out and die.'

Jack reached across the bar, pulled the barkeep closer. 'Whiskey. Think we'll need that big bottle you keep on the back wall there.'

For a moment it looked like the barkeep was going to protest, but then seeing how his toughest regular was doing, he decided he'd better stay on the right side of Jack Donovan. 'On the house,' he said.

Jack broke the bottle's neck on the side of the bar, then emptied the contents onto the rooster's burning head and down his back, sending slashes of fire all over. That whiskey must've been near pure alcohol, the way I heard the flames leaped when Jack poured it onto him. The ceiling got singed and they say you can still see the mark today.

Right then, anyone else in the saloon was wise enough not to intervene. No one even had the courage to leave, in case Jack and his men thought they were going to fetch the law. Whatever happened here, it wasn't going to reach Winn Sommers' ears. So the rooster rolled around blindly, screaming and flapping at his burning head and clothes and no one lifted a finger to help.

'Reckon that might do it,' Jack said. He had to speak loud to be heard over the guy's screams and the roar of the flames.

'Want us to put it out?' Joad said. 'Don't want to burn the saloon down, else where we gonna drink?'

'I think he'd be obliged if you did just that, Joad. Barkeep most likely would, too.'

Joad nodded at Spike to come give him a hand. Spike had been sitting at the corner table they'd taken to calling their own, and now he strode across the saloon, picked up a nearby table that a couple of guys had been studiously playing dominoes on, snapped off the tabletop, and with a few swift whacks, used that to stop the rooster moving. He knocked some teeth out too, but in the overall scheme of things, the rooster, now unconscious on the floor, didn't seem to mind. The fire was abating but his hair and clothes were still burning, so 'to put him out' Joad and Spike threw him through the window.

Whatever happened to that rooster, and they say he's still alive today, though bald as a coot with a burned head, he didn't come back to try his luck with Donovan again. In fact, after that day, nothing that could be taken the wrong way was said to Jack Donovan and his crew. Well, not until someone mentioned the jamboree show and how there was this cute as a button girl shooter who was said to be the fastest draw this side of the Missouri River. Quicker than all your famous gunslingers.

'That's a mighty big claim,' Jack said when he overheard this.

He, Joad and Spike had been sitting in their dark and dusky corner, letting the empties line up in front of them. Stale smoke hung in the air, a sour odour of rotgut now that they'd near run the bar dry.

The speaker shook his head quickly. 'Ain't saying it's true, Mr Donovan. Only what I heard. What they're saying about her.'

Jack had been chewing on baccy. He spat it out. There was straw on the floor. No need of a spittoon. He had a dangerous glint in his eye.

'Think we ought to go see about this,' he said. 'Fastest draw in the West?

I hate people advertising things that ain't true. I went there and paid any money I'd want a refund if she wasn't as quick as she's said to be.'

Joad put in, 'And there's the guy who runs it, about time we sorted him out.'

Spike dropped a hand on the table in assent.

Jack stood up. He didn't sway like a man who'd downed as much alcohol as he and his partners had downed. He hitched up his pants and pulled the front of his vest straight. His hat and jacket were on a coat-stand by the door, and as he left the saloon, Joad and Spike trailing after him, he pulled them on. When the men were gone a great weight lifted from the barroom.

A minute later, they were heading up Main and along First past the Chinerman, for the scrub where Daniel J. Roden's Travelling Medicine and Jamboree Show was gearing up for its afternoon business.

I don't need to tell you that all three were armed.

4

The show was going well. A lot of people were here, which was good news for a third straight day in the same town.

We weren't a big troupe, not like some of the others I'd seen on my travels with Danny's band. Others had exotic animals from overseas, including ostriches they raced in a circle like it was a derby, and they'd have boxing kangaroos that wore gloves and could punch a man out cold. That kind of show tended toward touring the bigger cities. There were also shows that would cross ours in the mid-sized towns. They carried your standard fare, like wrestling bears, and there were some had rides that they built up at each stop, spun you around and threw you up and down like a teeter-totter.

Daniel J. Roden's Travelling Medicine and Jamboree Show didn't have any of that, and since Clete had retired with his bad knee we didn't even have something we could pass off as a strong man or a wrestling challenge either.

But we had the medicine wagon with its 'patented soothe-all honey and sugar potion'. It came in varying grades, and did seem to ease a stricken throat or make a person feel a whole lot better with most of what was wrong with them. Didn't help out much if you got the squits, though; I'd learned that personally.

The medicine wagon was what brought in the real money, that and Danny's patter, his cowboy lasso tricks, Buck's knife-throwing and juggling act, and Smoke's shooting. Fortune reading wound up accumulating a trickle of coins. Wheat's singing was just a show-gatherer. Danny was our front-man and I'd never seen anyone who could turn a length of rope the way he did. He'd been fixing to teach me, but I was still struggling with the knots, so that they'd slip or hang tough or disappear altogether like they'd dissolved out of the rope. I was trying though.

Danny was into his routine now. He gave good, was expert at the patter. On the odd occasions I'd seen him miss a trick, he also had a line about that, how to get out of it.

'Well, I made a mistake there. Y'all will have noted how I never said I was perfect.' Then he'd grin a grin he wanted you to share in, pick up his rope and pull off whatever trick he'd just messed up — sometimes I think he made deliberate mistakes to get a crowd on his side — and say, 'Not perfect. But the best there is.'

I saw that he'd deliberately missed looping a volunteer out of the audience just now. He'd picked a good-looking young girl. He normally did if there was one available.

The audience had laughed when Danny's rope had fallen short, but they were laughing with him, and Danny was hanging his head in mock shame.

The girl was unsure if she should stay where she was or head back into the line of folks Danny had pulled her out of. 'Aw, shame,' someone said.

I knew what would happen next. And it did.

Danny waited till the girl turned around and kind of skipped-jogged her way to the crowd, mildly embarrassed. When she was about to join her family, and a considerable distance further away than when he'd missed looping her, he gave a couple of quick spins of his rope, buzzing it through the air, and then released it and spun it all the way out to her. Before she knew it, he lassoed her and twirled her around and pulled her in close to him, where, with her arms pulled in tight to her sides so she couldn't escape, he hid his and her face from the crowd with his hat and pretended to go in for a big kiss.

I'd seen the act a lot. Sometimes he got the kiss, sometimes he didn't.

Today he didn't. But that was OK, that was just the way it went. It was the showmanship that was important.

Danny finished up his act and I applauded along with everyone else.

'We're gonna take a few minutes now before Smoke Winters, Lady Sharp-shooter, comes out and entertains you all,' Danny said. 'Time enough for you folks to head on over to buy some refreshments or go to the medicine wagon where you can get a bottle of our best honey cure, just a few bits per bottle, a price that can't be beat anywhere. Soothes your throat, eases you through a cold, and although it won't cure a flu — I'm being honest with you here — it'll at least make you feel better while it lasts. Come on now, let's see you all buying in a bottle or two for the winter. Won't be another chance to get one 'fore spring when we all hope to come back and entertain you again.'

The show was for free, we didn't charge an admission price, but at the end of each performance it was my job to go around the crowd with a bucket to collect up any donations. Danny's act always did well. Usually the most money he'd get would be from the girl who he'd lassoed, and that was the case today, even though she hadn't kissed him.

I heard money clatter into the bucket really loudly when I presented it before her, and she had a mighty fine burn to her cheeks still. Her family had liked it all too, as had the rest of the crowd, and I had to use both hands to haul the bucket back to where Clete kept care of the money.

'Sho' looks like we had another good outing,' he said when I pushed my way behind the shady wagon.

'Not as heavy as yesterday, there's not as many people,' I said.

'We'll be moving out soon, no doubt.'

'Where'll we go next, Clete?'

'Danny's in charge, but we're running low on supplies, have to go and get some more cure-all fixed up. I figure we'll be headed over to one of his suppliers 'fore much longer.'

I left Clete tallying the bucket's load and went to call on Smoke. She was just coming out of the back of the wagon she shared with the fortune-teller. She was in her shooting outfit. I felt that swelling inside me at the sight of her.

'Luther,' she said, and gifted me a forced smile. She wasn't as happy as she had been earlier.

'Hi, Smoke. The main targets are set up, just gonna run out and put the extra ones in position. Danny got the audience up and ready, did a good old show.'

'And sent them to the wagon, I'm guessing.'

'Why, yes. And to the snack wagon. But I'm sure they'll be back.'

I'd seen a few familiar faces in the crowd today, and knew they'd come to see Smoke in her tight outfit again. I'd have come back too if I knew I'd only got so many days to see her. I said, 'You know Danny always shouts up a good trade for you, Smoke.'

'You go and see to the targets, Luther, I'll be along in a moment.'

I nodded, feeling like I'd said something out of turn, though I couldn't figure what that might be. I passed Danny, who was coming back from the medicine wagon, and he nodded at me. He'd a frown on his face, and I decided I probably would be wiser not speaking to him either.

★ ★ ★

I went out ready with the bucket again. I'd a couple of slices of fried tomatoes on a strip of paper. Gretchen Fry always kept a little something ready for when I got hungry, and although pickings had been thin of late, she made sure I didn't starve out completely.

'A growin' boy al'ays needs a little extra,' she'd say.

When the trouble began, I was sitting on the bucket, munching on my tomatoes, watching Smoke do some fast draws and trick shooting, swinging a

48

rifle around and making truly amazing shots no one else could make, and leading the applause when it was necessary.

Smoke had just emptied her pistols into a playing card target, and invited a volunteer — she'd picked an older man who lacked some in the teeth department — to do this. Unlike Danny, Smoke had a tendency to stick to picking out the local who'd been unfortunate when it came to handing out the looks. This guy was called Jeb; his eyes didn't point the same way, and his nose bent away to one side like he should turn his face that way to catch up to it.

'Now how many bullet holes do we see in that card, Jeb?' Smoke asked.

Jeb shook his head and said, 'Well, it's just the one, ma'am.' He added real apologetically, 'I guess you only hit it the one time.'

'Would you like to take the card off the mount then look behind there and tell me how many bullets are in the cork, Jeb?'

Jeb picked up the big card, unfastening the pegs I'd used to clip it on, and looked behind. This was a trick, similar to the one Smoke did when she'd get a guy to stand with a match sticking from his mouth and shoot the flame out. Smoke didn't have to get too close to that lucifer to put it out. The passage of the bullet would blow it out, and if that didn't do it, then the sigh of relief from the feller whose lips were in danger would do the job when he found out his head hadn't been shot off.

'Well, I'll be . . . There's six there! Six bullets,' Jeb said, turning the cork so everyone could see.

I applauded with everyone else, even though I was wise to this trick. Smoke only had to put one hole in the card, round about the middle of the mark, then miss the target intentionally, so it looked like she'd put each bullet in the same place. Jeb was displaying bullets pre-loaded into the cork before Smoke's show began.

'Yee haw,' a couple of guys shouted in

the audience, real appreciation there.

Now I don't want to make this sound like Smoke wasn't the real deal when it came to shooting; she surely was. But she couldn't do impossible things like putting six rounds into one bullet hole. Except maybe when she was at her best with a rifle, I wouldn't rule it out then. From a distance, with a rifle, she was the best I'd seen and the best I'd ever heard about. But making a shooting show out of rifle tricks is hard work. Everything's at a distance and no one really wants to stand 300 feet away from the shooter to see the target get pulped. Hence all the chicanery with the pistols. Showmanship, as Danny would say.

Smoke took her applause, spun her pistols, and was about to reload for the next part of her act, when Jack Donovan and his crew made themselves known.

'That's some mighty fine pistols you got there, lady. The pearl grips and all. I see the metal's nicely polished. And I say your outfit's fine enough to keep anyone happy if you did miss.'

He stepped out of the crowd, a big man draped in sour shadows and thunderclouds. You could sense the way folks moved away from him, like they were scared of being struck by lightning. Already some people were turning and leaving the show, hustling their kids on before them.

Smoke must've recognized him for the guy who'd given Danny trouble the other day. She didn't alter the expression on her face, but she paused in the act of reloading.

'That's sweet of you to say,' she said. But the friendliness in her voice was gone, and I knew it. Not only that: she knew it, and the crowd knew it. 'Wanna watch me do the next trick, see if I'm worth it?'

'Ain't seen nothing to impress me so far. You're OK on the quick draw, but I feel like I've been cheated. You ain't the fastest in the West, that I promise you.'

Jack Donovan heaved the weighty

skirts of his greatcoat aside so that his own pistols were visible. Like Smoke he had heavy iron hanging off either hip. A nervous hush spread through the people watching.

I looked around, hoping Danny or Clete — or one of the other guys, maybe Buck with his throwing knives — was about. I didn't see anyone, though. Buck would be suiting up to get ready for his routine, I realized. Wheat would be at the medicine wagon, because that's where the money was, to make sure nothing went missing. He'd already done his singing.

Smoke still hadn't loaded her pistols. Instead she holstered them with the chambers all but empty. She'd maybe had time to slot one bullet in there.

The nice easy atmosphere of the show had turned dark.

She cocked a hip, and tilted her head on one side.

'Well, now,' she said, trying not to be nervous. 'Ladies and gentlemen, looks like we've got a genuine gunslinger

53

here. Say, Mr Gunslinger, why don't you introduce yourself, come on over here and entertain the folks with some shooting? You just seen what I did, how about you show us how good you are? Luther, you all fix up another of the cards on a target for this gentleman.'

I stood up. My legs were tensed.

Jack Donovan didn't take his stare off Smoke.

'Ain't got no time for tricks, lady. I draw my guns, then it's to do business.'

'Smoke,' I said. 'You still want me to . . . ?'

She didn't take her eyes off Jack, but she waved me quiet. 'Then I don't know what you're doing, sir. Why you're interrupting the show.'

Silent Spike and Joad had pushed through the thinning crowd now. The smarter people, fearing a shootout, had drifted away, leaving some hesitant looking people behind. I didn't like the idea of there just being me and Smoke to deal with Donovan's crew if everyone up and left. I didn't even have a hammer this time.

'I'm interrupting the so-called show because I feel cheated,' Jack said.

'That right? Well, I'm mighty sorry to hear that.' Smoke was speaking softly now.

'Came here to see the lady sharp-shooter, fastest draw in the West. And got you instead. All feels a bit unobliging, you don't mind me saying.'

'I'm sorry to hear that. Maybe Luther can offer you something for free off the food stand, make up for you having to walk all the way from wherever it is you've come from to be here.'

Jack Donovan smiled and shook his head. He let a long stringy spit of baccy out to the ground. Wiping off his chin with the rear of a hand, he said, 'I don't think that's gonna cut it, ma'am.'

'Then what can we do for you?' Smoke said.

By now the crowd was severely diminished. A few of the last men still here considered staying, I saw it in their eyes, but when Spike and Joad stepped forward and showed their gunbelts, they saw the wisdom in not trying to fend off what now looked like the inevitable. Somebody was going to get hurt here and they didn't want it to be them.

'Ain't nothing you can do to heal my hurt now,' Jack said. 'I've been offended, and it wounds a man's pride to suffer such an offence. See, I'd come here all humble, waiting to look at someone draw a weapon and shoot faster than . . . oh, faster than, say, I can. And it ain't happened. I feel like I been . . . ' he made a show of hunting out a fancy word I figured he already knew and came out with, ' . . . debased.'

I found a way to speak around the obstruction that'd been growing in my throat.

'Mister, please, we don't want any trouble.'

'Hush up, boy. I seen you before and don't you think I forgot that.'

'Luther, go find Danny, Buck and

Clete,' Smoke said.

I turned to go but Spike was there, like a mountain before me. I almost bounced off him as I started out to fetch Danny. Instead he gripped me by the upper arm and I couldn't move.

I thought about shouting but didn't want to set things off. Right now things seemed to be balanced on some tipping point. I stared up into Spike's face but couldn't read anything human there. I thought about what Clete had said, about the way the West drew out wolves that looked like men.

'What say we keep this between you and me?' Jack Donovan said to Smoke.

'My guns aren't loaded,' Smoke said.

'Saw you fit one round in there before you holstered,' Jack Donovan said. 'You as good as you advertise yourself, you only need one.'

'There's three of you.'

'But there's only me saying I'm faster.'

'And I don't know which chamber the bullet's in. Might have to shoot five times before I land on the right one.'

Jack nodded. 'That's true.'

'And if I shoot you down,' Smoke said, 'I'm not convinced your friends will just pick you up and walk away. I don't want to get into a drawing contest with you.'

'Everybody hear that?' Jack said loudly. 'She says she can't take me.'

'That ain't what she said,' someone in what was left of the crowd (now dwindled to about eight or nine people, boys, a couple of women looking nervous, and unsure men) called. 'She said she didn't want to get into a contest with you. Didn't say she couldn't beat you.'

I expected Donovan to anger up at that, but he didn't. He had that calm about him, the same air I'd seen when he was pressing on Danny to hand over money. This was the kind of situation he lived for. He didn't have no nerves. I don't think he felt much of anything. He just had wants and desires. It came to me then that he wanted to shoot

Smoke. Not because she was a girl, not because she was pretty. But because he wanted to see some pain. He desired blood.

Doing my best, I tried to wrestle free of Spike, but he wasn't having it. 'Leggo,' I hissed. He glared at me and I kicked him in the shin.

He slapped me, a backhanded one that knocked me down. When I looked up, my whole head throbbed, and my lips and cheek and the thick of my nose felt about three times too large for my face.

Groggy, I did my best to scramble up and move out of his reach but the world lurched around drunkenly.

'I'll get Danny,' I called to Smoke and hitched up ready to run just as I heard a buzzing in the air.

That was when Jack Donovan pulled his guns.

He was fast, oh-so-fast as you wouldn't believe, and yes, I believe he was faster than Smoke. He brought both his pistols up, the one in his left hand levelling out at me, and I'd no doubt at all that he was going to pull on that trigger and blow my heart out of my body. The gun in his right hand was already locked onto Smoke.

But Smoke wasn't standing still. She ducked to her right, drawing her pistol.

Donovan fired off at her at the same time he pulled the trigger to end my life.

And it would've happened, I've no doubt about it. Both Smoke and me would be dead, or at the very least bleeding out with a bullet each in us, but for Daniel J. Roden.

That buzzing I'd heard. It was a rope being spun and let loose.

5

Danny's lasso came down around Jack Donovan, squeezing his arms to his sides just as the gunslinger pulled the triggers. The roar from the gunfire rose into the air and bullets went winging off slantwise.

The people dumb enough not to have got out of there started running, and those already on their way picked up their pace too. Some screamed. In the chaos, I saw Clete coming over at a trot, the best he could do with his bad knee. His dark skin and size had him stand out from the folks fleeing in the opposite direction. But it was gonna take him a while to get here and I didn't think it was time we had on our side.

'The hell?' Donovan said as he tried to free himself enough to fire off another salvo.

Danny was trying to pull him over, but it backfired as a plan, 'cos it allowed Donovan to shrug the rope up and ease one of his arms free. And while he wasn't set squarely on his feet, he could still shoot.

Smoke had drawn, and now she fanned the hammer of her pistol. She had four dead clicks before the explosion that announced a shot came through.

Her bullet spat at Donovan, but because she was off balance too, and because Donovan had been spun around trying to unhinge himself from Danny's rope, the bullet only nicked his side, tearing a rip in his greatcoat.

At least it meant he only got one round off at Danny before he had to reassess the threat Smoke posed to him.

Danny dropped to the floor, fearing more bullets, but he didn't let go his rope. He pulled on it, hard. Still without a steady stance, Donovan turned to finish off Smoke, who was considerably nearer than Danny and an open target. She flung her gun at him, one of the tricks she never usually performed with the show pistols, and it flew straight into his face. It was enough to make him grimace and shake his head. More importantly, it gave her a chance to scramble along the rough grass, take cover behind a nearby barrel upon which her rifle rested.

I kicked out at Spike again, this time going for that spot between his legs, not caring that this was underhand fighting. If Clete could do it on that wrestler, then I could do it now.

Spike had been reaching across his waist for his own gun, which he wore opposite his shooting hand with the pistol grip sticking out backwards.

I must've got him good in the meats, because he opened his mouth and let out a silent wail, doubled up with the pistol in his hand, and wasn't in a position to sight on Smoke or Danny. He punched out at me but it was a lacklustre strike and missed. I ducked back and grabbed the iron bucket on which I'd been sitting earlier, swung it over in the air and clanged it into his ugly whiskered face.

His hat came off as he went the rest of the way over, and because I'd swung it that hard and fast I near all but fell after the bucket. Dented the darn thing too, but I didn't think Clete would give me a roasting for it.

That guy's jaw must've been made out of stone though, because he got up real quick, a sneer across his face, half of which was red from where the bucket struck. He shook himself right, raised his gun and sighted on me.

A hole opened up before me, big and empty, the end of the gun barrel eclipsing the world. Everything fell silent, all colour left my eyes. This was the last thing I'd see, a darkness bigger than life, about to swallow me.

A couple of slow heartbeats calmed me, and a reluctant kind of an acceptance touched me. If this was the end, then this was the end. Maybe I'd see Ma and Pa again, Stephanie too. A haunting song played through my flesh as I was about to bid life goodbye and find out if anything happened after death.

But I never did get to learn about that. I was saved.

This time it wasn't Danny's rope did the job. Clete did, bashing into Spike and rolling away with him. Both were big men and it was a real clash. Clete had wrestling experience, but Spike was one of those wolves Clete had talked about, not a feeling in his bones or need in his heart that wasn't connected with his own betterment and satisfaction. Plus, he was a good twenty years younger.

I gasped heavily, the world rushing back at me in intimate focus. But I could still see the vast emptiness of the gun barrel into which I'd just looked. It was like it had sucked half of my mind into it, because I was having to think around its dark emptiness now, come to terms with the fact I wasn't dead.

When I did get some thoughts clear,

a kind of worried inspiration took over me, and I found myself hunting to see what Joad was up to. He'd been in the thicker part of the crowd when he'd stepped forward, and had moved into a clear area for himself. He'd got his gun — a long barrelled Colt — drawn, and was swinging the weapon between Danny and Smoke. Only problem for him was that Danny was still yanking on Jack Donovan enough to be steering him from side to side, despite Donovan's shots firing off, and Joad couldn't get a clear bead on Danny because his boss was in the way. Smoke was hidden behind the barrel, working on her rifle.

Buck and Wheat were coming from the other wagons now, and they were armed. Rifles each. Wheat was accompanied by a deputy and he was hollering for the shooting to stop. Donovan heard this, snarled as he finally fought his way free of Danny's rope, and brought his gun up.

He took a shot at the deputy, which straight away was a hanging offence. No two ways about it. You shot at a deputy, you were set to swing.

Donovan's only good shot of the day went into that deputy, took his face out from in front of his head and pushed it right the way through to the back and out onto the ground behind him. Something grey and spotted that must've been his brain went with it. Somehow it left the deputy's hat on and he even kept running, the way I'd seen a decapitated chicken run, before flopping in a lifeless bundle to the ground. On a day full of trick shooting, that was one trick I wished I'd never seen.

'You killed a deputy,' Danny yelled at Donovan.

'Kill you too,' Donovan shouted. But his guns clicked on empty as he levelled at Danny.

Now that Donovan wasn't being pulled in a merry dance, Joad made his choice and shot at Danny, missed, then aimed at Smoke, pinning her down behind the barrel she was behind.

Under fire from Joad, she couldn't get a clear shot at any of the gunslingers. That was a heck of a pity, because right now we needed Smoke with a clear shot with that rifle. Three bullets would end the lives of all three of these men; I knew it. Quick with pistols, she was lightning with a rifle. She never missed.

Joad fired into the barrel she hid behind at his leisure. She couldn't level her rifle before he'd hit her. Joad was too far off for me to help Smoke any, and Danny was pulling his rope back ready to spin up into the air and try to do something. Wheat and Buck were as hampered in taking shots at Donovan as Joad had been taking shots at Danny. This time because Danny was between them and Donovan.

Clete was taking some punches off Silent Spike, so I ran into the gunslinger. He'd dropped his weapon, and I suppose if I'd been smarter I'd've picked it up and tried to shoot him and then point over in Joad's direction. But I'd only ever held Smoke's pistols when

I'd been cleaning them, on the promise that one day she'd teach me to draw and shoot . . . only first of all I had to learn to do the tricks Danny could do with his rope, and I wasn't fast on learning the first one yet.

So I barrelled into Spike, hard enough to tilt him over before I was sent sprawling by an elbow in my chest. Clete got a whumping fist in of his own, and Spike went the rest of the way over. Clete's face was bloodied. One of his eyes was swelling shut, but he wasn't done yet.

Like he was a wrestling bear himself, he turned on all fours and started at Spike. Spike backed up, rising to his feet, and I think if he'd had a voice he'd'a called Clete a whole bunch of names at this point, mostly related to his ancestry and the state of his mental health.

But he didn't, so all we could see was his face screwing up as he pushed hisself away and started in for where he'd dropped his gun. By now the guys from the wagon had taken good defensive positions and couldn't be caught by gunfire, and Danny was with them, so they shot at Joad and Donovan.

Joad called to his friends, 'Let's go, guys. We gotta quit. Too much fire-power.'

His weapons still empty, Donovan ran after Joad, ducking low to avoid being picked out by any one shot. As he rounded the corner of the stables, Spike followed after him, and jerked in a mighty spasm, so that I thought he was gonna fall on the ground with his life leaking out of him. But he only hitched up a moment before carrying on in a stagger.

When I looked around to see who'd got him, I saw Smoke standing beside the water barrel, the end of her rifle curling wisps of blue ribbons into the air.

I offered Clete a hand. But he just shook his head, moaned, and said, 'Water. Go fetch me some water.'

Clete's face aside, the show crew had somehow come away unharmed.

★   ★   ★

Jack Donovan and his men shot another deputy that day; killed him outright too. As they were chased out to the edges of town, they also hit the sheriff, good enough to set off a lot of cussing from Winn Sommers. But there were enough men who'd joined in to help the law by this point that it wasn't the end of things. With his wounds bleeding freely, Winn Sommers had pinned Donovan and his men down in a large painted house at the end of Prairie Lane. The house belonged to one of the town's wealthier families, and there were people in it when Donovan's crew entered. It was shingled on the roof, had a wrap-around porch, and sat in a pretty garden. Donovan and his men bust out the glass in windows upstairs and down, so they could angle out their weapons and pick off anyone who came close.

It looked like a standoff, with no one able to get to the house without being shot at, and no one being able to get away from the house without being put down.

The afternoon went kind of quiet for a while, the sheriff got bandaged up and stayed on site.

After a time, Jack Donovan stuck out a white flag of his own making — it was comprised of a pair of ladies' underwear and the leg of a kitchen stool — and requested a moment to talk to the sheriff.

Sommers agreed, and with his hands raised by his shoulders to show he wasn't gonna shoot anyone, limped to the edge of the walk as Donovan appeared on the porch with a little girl held in front of him.

'Deal's this,' Donovan told Winn, who looked pale and wan from blood loss. 'You bring three good, fed and watered horses out here, and we leave town unharmed. We get to the edge of town, go on a bit more, then we release the girl. This doesn't happen, we just remain in this standoff until we run out of food and then we shoot the girl and as many of you as we can.'

Seeing he didn't have any choice in the matter, Winn Sommers had three horses readied and watched Donovan and his men ride out of there as dusk was coming down. In the house, the girl's parents were found with their throats cut.

As agreed to by Sommers and Donovan, a couple of the local men followed the riders to the edge of town, making sure to keep a good distance so there'd be no gunfire, and then went on beyond as Donovan and his crew kept going. The men reported that once they were beyond shooting range of town, Donovan's group had dropped something in the river — it was hard to tell what, but they thought it was the little girl — kicked those horses into a gallop and disappeared into the night.

Well, the men rushed to the river. It wasn't swollen or fast flowing, which was a mercy, but it was deep. Even in the poor light they could see that the bundle flowing downstream was motionless.

Fearing the girl had fainted or was unconscious from the tumble into the river, one of the men jumped in and swam out, had a mind to snag the bundle and turn it over.

It wasn't the girl. Just a set of sheets and blankets done up to fool someone at a distance.

Of the girl there was no sign. She hadn't been left further down the trail. She didn't walk into town of her own accord later. Donovan and his men had taken her with them.

Winn Sommers managed to nod and say, 'Someone's going to have to go after them and bring that little girl back,' before he slumped over and couldn't be woken, not even by the doctor who was attending to his gunshot wound.

6

It had been an uneasy night, and there'd been a lot of rumour going around as to what had happened and why it had happened. We kept mostly to ourselves, but one of the guys, Wheat Rayne, had wandered into town, found not many people were interested in talking to him.

'Weren't being openly discourteous,' he'd said on his return. (He was telling us all of this as we sat around a small fire, a stew bubbling away before us.) 'But they made it pretty clear there wouldn't have been the trouble with Donovan if we hadn't come here.'

'I doubt that,' Danny said. 'Donovan's the kind of man who always gets around to raising trouble. People like him find a way.'

'That's how I saw it too,' Wheat said.

'Didn't seem politic to say as much though.'

'The sheriff?' Smoke said. 'How is he?' She'd been quiet since the afternoon. She'd taken off her shooting outfit and was in plain trousers and what I figured for one of Danny's shirts. It was too big for her. It made her look cute as all heck through.

'He's in a bad way,' Wheat said. 'Doc says the bullet nicked an artery, one of the big ones. All a question of stopping him bleeding out now. They do that, it's gonna be a long time before he's recovered enough to go back to his duties.'

Danny nodded. 'It's hard enough for him as it is. He lost both his deputies. Town's got no law enforcement at the moment.'

'Local marshal will probably come in, sit the jailhouse for a while, keep things under control. At least that's the idea I heard people talking up,' Wheat said.

'But the marshal can't look after the

town and go bring that little girl back,' Smoke said.

'No, I reckon not.'

'He'd have to send for more men, which will take more time. Donovan will be long gone by then.'

We sat around the fire some more, watching the flames turn and dance, not really saying much of anything. When we wanted, we took a ladle to the stew Gretchen Fry had cooked up and ate out of tin bowls. The stew was hare and the meat was tough. But it tasted good. Maybe anything would after you'd looked down the barrel of a gun.

Not long after the fire started to die down, we started off to bed. I'd been sleeping under the wagon I usually shared with Clete, on account of it being warm enough to do so, and I decided it was safe to carry on with that tonight, what with Donovan and his crew out of town.

I was woken deep into the night by voices, soft and low, but carrying easily.

I started awake, my heart running like a jackrabbit, until I realized it was just Smoke and Danny.

'Stay,' Danny was saying. 'Just this one night. We don't have to . . . you know. Again. Just stay.'

'I can't, Danny. You know I don't want anyone to know.'

'Who's gonna care? Anyone with two bits to their name can work it out.'

'I don't care if people make a guess,' Smoke whispered. 'It's not the same.'

'No one's gonna say anything. Hell, you been wearing my shirt all afternoon. What's that tell folks?'

'I say we're wrong to go tomorrow,' Smoke said. Her feet were bare. She had wonderful ankles, so graceful. And her legs went up a long way. I inched forward, keeping in the shadows behind the wagon wheel, so I could see better.

Danny wore only his undergarments. Smoke stood at the foot of his wagon, a blanket wrapped around her. I don't

78

know that she had much on underneath it. She was carrying her clothes in one arm.

I figured they were arguing over something other than them being found together, and it took me a while to realize what.

'We gotta leave,' Danny said. 'There's nothing else for us here. You heard what Wheat said. And we was planning on moving on anyway, you know that. Jack Donovan or not.'

'That little girl — '

'I told you, she's not our concern.'

'She oughta be someone's.'

'It's the law. The marshal will deal with it.'

'You don't have any idea,' Smoke said, and turned away from him.

He hissed her name but she didn't reply. She strode over to the wagon she shared with Cara Treene and crept in as quietly as she could. Danny cursed, stood around at the entrance to his own wagon a while, spat and then went back inside.

* ★ ★

We heard the next day that Winn Sommers had died, just as we were about done loading everything on board the wagons. I'd pulled up the tall thin posts that marked the entrance to the show and wiped the points clean. Clete, his face all puffed up, and with him moving around in a slow way 'cos of all his aches, showed me how to use a knife to keep the point sharp for when I'd have to plant them at the next place we stopped.

One of the locals came around to see us off. He wasn't a bad sort, and had drunk with Danny and Wheat in one of the saloons. He stood now with his hat in his hands, turning it around by the brim.

'Jack Donovan's crew took out all the law here. Selectmen are gonna meet later, look to appoint a new sheriff. Meantime, well, I don't know.' He kicked his heels in the scrub, looked up. 'Word's gone out to fetch down the marshal. Probably take a day or two to get here. When he arrives we'll tell him all that happened. If you gotta go, then you gotta go, but he'd probably like to hear your side of events.'

'There ain't nothing we can tell him that anyone in the crowd couldn't tell him,' Danny said. 'Important stuff came after Donovan got driven off from here, when he shot the sheriff. Folks saw what happened to his first deputy here. We'd only be more voices saying the same thing.'

'I can't make you change your mind and stay?'

'Can't see any value in that.'

I looked at Smoke, who had her face set in a way that didn't allow you to read any emotion. She wasn't happy though, I knew that. And after what I'd overheard last night, and what I'd seen . . .

She and Danny must be lovers, and for who knew how long. But she wasn't happy with his decision to go now. Though quite what she expected us to do about the kidnapped girl, I didn't know.

I'd asked Clete about what the men might do to her while I'd sharpened the points on the fence posts, and he'd shaken his head.

'Not something you want to think about, Luther. Make sure you glide that knife to make those cuts straight.'

'But Smoke's not happy. Last night, I saw her coming out of Danny's — '

'Whoa now. You hush up there.'

Clete had a finger out to me. He sounded angry, and he was rare to find a temper.

'What Danny and Smoke do on a night ain't no account of yours, Luther Jay Connolly.'

I hung my head. 'Well, I'm sorry,' I said. 'But I overheard them arguing — '

'You did, did you? And they knew you were listening in?'

'No, sir.'

'And you didn't let them know you were there?'

'I didn't get the chance.'

'And you'd've taken it if it was there, am I right? No, I didn't think so. You know I was the one brought Smoke up, mostly, don't you?'

This was new to me. I knew Smoke and Clete were close, but I hadn't heard this before.

'Back when I was in the cavalry, fighting the Sioux in the Indian wars, the Negro divisions got sent in to do a lot of the dirtier fighting. You don't read much about it in the history books. To believe those books, you'd think there wasn't ever an African in the cavalry. But that's not true. Anyhow, we did us the dirty fighting, like I say, and just as I got hurt in the knee, we came up on a place near Box Canyon out in the wilds, found a small settlement of Indian tents. You know what they call them, all standing upright, a circle of teepees. Weren't no men around when we rode in. All the warrior braves had been killed. In we came, a dusty old bunch we must've made, all of us dark skinned, and there she was among the

Indians, this little white girl with the brightest hair you ever saw.'

'Smoke,' I said. 'She told me she used to have dark hair, when she was really little. It's one of the few things she ever says about herself. I told her I like it how it is now, makes her special, different.'

'Some people have a big enough fright, it can make their hair turn. Happens overnight. You hear about it.'

'That happened to Smoke, Clete?'

'She was taken from her family, saw them murdered right before her eyes, her daddy scalped, her mommy . . . well, best not to talk about what happened to her mommy. But she was small, maybe five years old. When I found her she was ten, maybe eleven. Hard to tell her real age.'

I didn't know what to say. Smoke had never said anything about this to me. I wondered if Danny knew.

'Indians traded her between tribes, till one set brought her up as one of their own. I'd heard tales of it happening before. But this was the first time I'd seen it.'

'What did you do?'

'Well, I'd caught my knee that week and it wasn't fixing right, didn't have no option but to resign my commission, as the officers say.' Clete smiled wryly at that, then said, 'Because no one knew what to do with her, I took that girl out of there too. Started wrestling in shows when my knee could stand it, brought Smoke up as best I could, got her talking English again. She started learning to shoot, taught by a trick shooter who was faster than anyone I ever saw, including Jack Donovan. Went from show to show, and here we are with Danny now.'

'And Smoke wants us to go after that girl, even though we don't owe her or her family nothing.'

'That's right.'

'You reckon it's because of what happened to Smoke when she was a little girl?' I said. 'Seeing her ma and pa die.'

Clete chewed on a thought a moment. 'You saw your ma and pa die, but you ain't hurting to go after the girl.'

'My hair's the same colour as it was back then,' I said.

'And you weren't kidnapped by Indians. I recollect correctly, you was happy joining Danny's show.'

'So it's complicated,' I said.

'It is,' Clete agreed. 'But I got nothing but the best hopes for that girl, don't want you talking about her behind her back. She does what she does with who she likes and that's her business. And it could be worse business than Danny Roden.'

'What if no one goes after Donovan?'

To that, Clete didn't have an answer. He told me to get back to shaving the points of the posts and I suddenly found myself worrying about Smoke. It was a good thing we were moving out tomorrow. It wouldn't allow Smoke the time to get a crazy notion into her head and go after Donovan by herself.

86

7

We hitched up and lit out of Bradbury, aiming to take a wide turn north and call in on a couple of towns skirting the mountains on the edge of the Great Plains, one-street settlements that didn't have much beyond a saloon and a hotel with whores in the upstairs rooms. Sort of place a cowboy or prospector would ride into for a night and then leave the next morning. Danny said it was worth stopping just to unload what was left of the honey soothe-all, and they was places we ain't never been to before.

I rode with Smoke for a time, sitting beside her, tried to get her talking. But she answered with one word or two, never anything more, and I fell into silence as the wagon bucked and rocked.

The second night we set up camp

between towns and I slept under Clete's wagon again. It was a clear night. The sky was filled with stars and you could hear the insects creaking. The air smelled of distant thunder, a tang that lit up the sinuses, but there were no clouds. A lighted lamp hung from the back of Danny's wagon, and I saw him peer out every so often. At first I figured he wasn't sleeping well, and then realized the lamp must have been left for Smoke. When he understood she wasn't going to be joining him, he reached up and took it down, put it out, and with a sigh went inside to try and sleep.

I was pondering on Smoke's history. Thinking about her being taken from her parents and knowing that she'd never see them again made me tear up and I thought about my own ma and pa, the farm, and even that useless old mule Horace. I couldn't work out on God's plans, why he should take Ma and Pa and yet leave Jack Donovan and his friends alive.

Wasn't a manly thing to do, but I sobbed silently under that wagon until I'd exhausted myself so thoroughly that when Smoke did get up and go about her business, I didn't scent a whiff of what she was about. Didn't hear her saddle up a horse, load her things, and leave. I was stone asleep.

The first I knew she'd gone was in the morning, when people raised their voices and called for her.

'Smoke?' I said, peering out from under the wagon through sleep-tired eyes.

Danny was striding back and forth, calling her name. Cara Treene stood silently, looking around, as if she might use that supposed third eye of hers to see what no one else could see. Buck came back from where the horses had been tethered for the night.

'That dun's gone, Danny.'

Danny nodded, and I don't think I'd ever seen him look so dismayed in all the time I'd known him.

'The one Smoke had a favouring for,' he said.

I saw Clete's face. He looked so sad, and even though his hair had been greying a while, I swear that the dark ones were crinkling away to be replaced by more frost right now.

'It's about that little girl,' he said.

But of course, there weren't none of us hadn't worked that out already.

'Can't force her back, Danny,' Clete told him.

'I don't care what you say I can or can't do, Clete. She ain't going after that child.'

'You ain't her master, don't you forget that.'

'And don't you forget who pays you out a wage, old man. I say we're going after her, we're going after her.'

'It's like that, is it?' Clete said.

'It is.'

'You can bring her back, but it won't stop her being who she is or make her yours,' Clete said. 'You think on that.'

We didn't spare any time cooking up a fire and making breakfast. Danny ran around calling on everyone to hitch up the horses. Wheat, who sometimes liked to ride one of the duns himself, singing as he went, settled for riding on a wagon, while Danny and Buck worked at turning us all around. Pretty soon we were heading toward Bradbury.

We were going back, chasing not after Jack Donovan and the little girl he'd kidnapped, but after Smoke. We were a horse down but Danny didn't seem to care. He led from his wagon, pushing on faster than a sensible man would have ridden.

Eventually, with the horses puffing and starting to rear back and stagger, he listened to Buck's warnings and pulled on the reins. 'Whoa, there.'

We all slowed down and there was nothing but the creak of the wagons settling, the horses snorting and blowing, and the expectation of what might happen next.

'Need a break,' Clete said. I was

sitting beside him. He had settled for looping his braces over his shoulders without an undershirt, and you could see the sweat on his skin, like dew on the bark of an oak tree. Clete was mighty aromatic today. Of course, not a one of us must have smelled all that good. We'd not had time to go about our morning ablutions the way we would have liked.

'Horses can't take this kind of travelling across this kind of country,' Clete said.

'You gonna tell him?' I said.

'He knows,' Clete said.

We sat waiting. Danny did the right thing and called a break, but you could hear the unhappiness about the fact in his voice.

'We'll stop here for a while, let the horses get their breath back.'

'Amen,' Wheat called to that.

Danny didn't say anything. He hung his head.

★   ★   ★

We got to Bradbury late afternoon. Like before, we were tired from the ride, but this time we didn't make a pretence of drumming up trade for a show. People recognized the carts and wagons, watched us from stoops and porches and along the boardwalks lining the dusty road leading to Main Street, where the hard-pack made the going a little easier.

I didn't feel at ease. Bradbury wasn't the sunny town we'd come to before. There'd been shootings and death, and the Lord alone knew what had happened to that poor little girl that was taken from them. I realized I didn't even know her name.

'Where we gonna hitch up?' Buck asked from his horse.

'Same as before,' Danny said.

We passed the hotel and the bank, and I nodded at the Chinerman standing beside his big tea urn. He was in the process of cleaning up his tin mugs for the day, probably figuring he wouldn't have any more customers. His face, always hard to read, didn't tell me anything as he watched us go by and turn off to pass down by the livery stables. If he was pleased we were back and might be buying off of him or not, I really couldn't tell.

At least I didn't have to dig in and pound the posts into the earth this time. My back stiff from all the riding, I walked around trying to ease my aches and pains. Others were doing the same. Danny called at Wheat to see to it that everyone was all right and then strode off into the town.

'Go after him,' Clete told me. 'Make sure he knows we're on his side. And try to make sure he doesn't do anything stupid.'

'Why me?' I said. 'Wouldn't it be better if you went?'

'You're a youngster. Danny's many things, and sometimes he's a weak man, but he knows how to set an example. You around, he'll act proper, showing you how it should be done . . . if his feelings don't get the better of him.'

94

'All right,' I said, though I wasn't sure how much of what Clete said was true.

I picked up my pace and with more than a little trepidation went after Danny.

8

'Clete send you?' Danny said as I caught up with him.

'Yes, sir.'

Danny nodded.

He was pounding along the boardwalks towards the sheriff's office and he didn't slow up any just because I was with him. The sheriff's office was a stone building, beside a rundown frame rooming house with windows turned the silver of old wood. Opposite the rooming house was a hotel if you had the money to spend. It was painted a fresh blue, had a white sign with black lettering on it, all fancied up with a red drop shadow. By contrast the rooming house had a poor sign with the lettering flaking, and it hung from a swing attachment that creaked like the door in a haunted house. Of the two establishments, it was the quietest, a sign of how prosperous Bradbury had become.

'Stay close and don't say nothing, let me do the talking,' Danny said as he strode on.

'Yes, sir,' I said.

Danny squared his shoulders, knuckled his hat forward. He hadn't shaved today, and his wide jaw was dark with new whiskers.

'Say Danny, about you and Smoke,' I started. 'I was thinking about how long you two — '

Danny came to a sudden halt and I walked right past him. I had to turn around to look at him.

'You understand that bit about saying nothing?' His eyes bored into mine. 'I have to send you back to Clete now?'

'No, Danny. I'll hush up. Was only wondering something. I'm sorry.'

'Ain't nothing to wonder about.'

I felt like challenging him about it. But I was learning not to open my mouth and spill out every thought in my head. Something inside me had turned blue knowing Smoke and

Danny were riding the nights out together. I wasn't dumb enough to think I had any claim on Smoke. Any thoughts I had about her were juvenile fantasies, I guess, but it hurt all the same to know she wouldn't ever be mine. All I'd wanted to say was that I hoped she and Danny were happy.

Danny banged a fist on the hard wood of the sheriff's door. 'Hello, the jailhouse,' he called before pushing it open.

Inside there was a desk, on the wall was a row of rifles with a couple of spaces where missing weapons would go, to the side of the room was a pot-bellied stove and chimney pipe leading up through the ceiling. Lanterns hung on the rafters, and were lighted now, because the windows were small and mean and didn't look kindly on sunlight. In the back, there was a row of cells, with pallet beds inside and no windows. Three men were in the sheriff's office. Not one of them looked like he knew the front end of a gun from its back. They were standing around the desk, leafing through sheets of paper for something to do other than scratch their behinds.

'Who's in charge here?' Danny said.

The men looked at each other like they weren't sure. 'Ain't none of us legal deputies,' one said, stepping forward. He was greying, with a toothcomb moustache. He looked like he spent a lot of time outdoors so it was hard to judge his age accurately. The lines on his face could've been through hard living or an accumulation of the years. I guessed he was in his fifties; younger than Clete but with maybe fifteen years on Danny.

'Marshal not arrived yet?'

'Word's only just been sent for him. Won't be here another day at best.'

Danny sighed. But he'd not expected anything other, I reckoned. He'd said before we left Bradbury that it would take time to get a marshal involved.

'You're the showground man, ain't you?' one of the other fellows said. He wasn't much older than Danny, but he'd been living an easy life. He was soft and jowly, and he reminded me of Mr Turner, back in the lawyer's office when my pa's will was being read. 'What cause have you to return, sir? Your last visit wasn't exactly conducive to making the town a nicer place, if I remember.'

'That wasn't our doing and you know it.'

'Hadn't been a shooting in a good ten years before you arrived. Least not a murder shooting.'

'You came to the show, I remember you,' Danny said, eyeing him like a predator will its prey, finding its measure. 'Watched Smoke, the girl who did the shooting show. Came back two days in a row afterwards.'

I didn't know if it was true or not, there was a good chance Danny was guessing because a lot of men came to the show to see Smoke shoot, but the soft man's cheeks burned up a little and he put on an affronted air.

'A man can watch a show, can't he? I thought that was what you wanted.'

'Don't recall you were so keen to be in the audience for my performances.' Danny smiled, knowing exactly why he'd been to Smoke's trick shooting show. Same reason I supposed I'd have gone back. To watch her in her tight outfit, and maybe hoping she'd pick you out of the crowd to flirt with and do her trick shooting.

'She came back here, didn't she?' Danny said. 'You seen her? She'd have to ask around, talk about which direction Jack Donovan and his men went. Where is she?'

The men exchanged looks.

Danny was wearing a gunbelt. I'd not seen him take to putting one of those on very often. If Danny wore a gun it was for protection, while we were riding the more lawless parts of the country. But the way he wore it now, I thought it made him look angry and dangerous.

I decided to remind him I was there,

so his temper wouldn't rise and get the better of him.

'You should tell us if she has been here,' I said to the men. 'We're not looking to cause trouble. We just want to see she's safe. She's one of ours and we look after our own.'

The older man considered this, then nodded.

'Don't see there's harm in telling you. She's gone anyway. You missed her.'

'Then she was here,' Danny said, his voice a mixture of relief and tension.

'Just told you that, ain't I? But she's gone now.'

'Gone where?' I said before Danny could ask. He flashed me an irritated look and by nodding at him I allowed that I'd stay quiet from now on.

'She left with Bobby Lee Parker not three hours ago.'

Danny and I looked at each other. Neither one of us had heard of him.

'Who's this Bobby Lee Parker?' Danny said.

'Little girl who went missing, he's her uncle. Last kin she's got living now that Donovan and his men killed his sister and her husband.'

'What kind of man is he?'

'He's a fool is what he is,' someone said from behind us. We both turned around, Danny's hand close to the grip of his pistol.

An older man stood just outside the door. He wore a tailored suit and a white shirt with one of those big frilly ruffs up the front. A black string tie hung down his front like rats' tails set off the brilliance of the shirt, even though he was standing under the porch roof and the light didn't reach under it too well.

'A well-meaning fool,' he said, elaborating. 'But a fool all the same.'

He stepped inside. His hat was in one hand and he reached out to shake Danny's hand with the other. I saw Danny's eyes glance down to this newcomer's sides looking for a weapon before he reached out to shake.

'Sampson Hannah,' the man said. 'Local sawbones and all around curer of ailments. Of course, I don't have the benefits of your miraculous cure-all, so I can't fix everyone who's under the weather. But I do my best and have done for a while now.'

Dr Hannah had been the name I recollected Wheat mentioning when the sheriff had been shot. He'd worked hard on him by accounts, got him as settled as he could, but in the end he'd failed to save him.

'This Parker, he's a fool how?' Danny said.

Doc Hannah smoothed back his hair. He wore a troubled expression. 'Bobby Parker is a good man. He's good for hunting in the woods, can bring back a rabbit or a string full of squirrels. He was good for his marriage too. But he lost his wife a couple of seasons ago to a particularly vicious infection. Nothing he could do about it. Nothing I could do about it. Since then he's become somewhat reckless and has taken to drinking more than he should, and he spends too long in church praying for a miracle to bring his Elisabeth back. Underneath everything he's a man with a good heart. But good hearts don't always make wise minds.'

'And Parker's kin to the little girl who was taken,' Danny said, 'so he feels he ought to go out and bring her back?'

'Bobby and his wife never had any children. Wasn't for want of trying. But it never happened for them. Perhaps Bobby feels that not only is it his duty to go and fetch little Mary-Ann back, but also that in some mysterious way it was all intended to be. Part of a bigger plan.'

'Why'd he wait for Smoke to turn up if he had this idea it was his duty to go bring the little girl back?'

The doctor dipped his head, and the grey-haired gentleman beside the sheriff's desk spoke up.

'Because he only got sober enough to understand what had happened to his niece today, that's why. Then your girl rode into town, started asking where the posse was and if she could join in. Of course, until the marshal comes, no one's looking at herding up a posse.'

He'd the grace to look a mite embarrassed by this, I saw.

'Did Bob — uh, Mr Parker, did he try to round up a posse?' I said.

'A drunk man couldn't round up a posse, son,' the grey-haired man said.

'But he tried. And no one answered his call,' I said, sure that this was true.

'Your girl rode in and got to talking to Bobby Lee,' the softer man said.

'And she was the only one who would help,' I said. I was angry at the cowardice of the whole town, and at these men here who wouldn't own up to their yellow streaks. I kept my voice level, like I imagined Clete would do in the situation. 'You did nothing.'

'We warned them it wasn't too bright an idea until the marshal came in. Then we could round up a proper posse to go and do it, maybe even hire in some professional gunhands.'

'In the meantime,' Danny said, 'while you sit around doing nothing, there's no telling what could have happened to that little girl, Mary-Ann.'

'Now look. Like I tried to explain to the boy,' the older man said to Danny, 'until the marshal gets here . . . '

Dr Hannah spoke at this point. He didn't raise his voice. He'd no need to. 'I think we all know the situation, Virgil.'

The one called Virgil set his cheeks in an expression like stone. He wasn't going to give.

'So Smoke and this Bobby Lee Parker, they've gone after Donovan together,' Danny said. 'They have a clue where he's gone?'

The men exchanged another look.

'Where'd they go?' Danny said. 'You have an idea, I can see it in you.'

'You'd hope they'd go to the only place that would have them,' the older man, this Virgil, said with a sigh. 'It's the only chance the little girl has. If they've gone into the country, well that's it for her. They'll do what they do, then leave her. Alive or dead. No telling what's best for her in that situation, alone and hungry and unable to feed herself.'

'This place that would take Donovan and the others in, that's where Smoke would have gone,' Danny said. 'She'd take the chance the girl's alive. So where is it, what's it called?'

Virgil spoke like a man passing on the news of a bereavement.

'They've gone to Inferno,' he said.

9

While Danny and I were in the sheriff's office, Smoke was riding the dun out along the old trails that Bobby Lee Parker reasoned would get them to Inferno as fast as possible. Bobby Lee was leading.

He was up at the top end of his thirties, a lean man with a long moustache and thinning hair. He had smudgy eyebrows and an old dove-grey Stetson that had known better days and probably better heads to sit upon. He rode a chestnut brown mare whose saddle was filled with rifles in sheaths and canteens rolling with water. He had a roll blanket and jerky in his bags.

They carried on along the passes, flitting in and out of woodland, and followed old trackers' routes, which Bobby said was a gamble to save them time, as long as they didn't come across some hurdle or other. Luck was with them, in this at least, and they made good passage.

Now, as the sky turned from a luminescent turquoise to a darker blue with the dipping of the sun, and clouds started to pile like rubble at the coming of night, they were only a couple miles out from Inferno.

'It's too dark to go any further,' Smoke said.

'But we got to rescue Mary-Ann,' Bobby Lee argued.

He looked tired. Even in the waning light, you could tell his eyes were weighted down by exhaustion and a life too long without focus. Now he'd got something to hold onto, a reason to live again. Smoke was coming to realize this was a dangerous combination, and that Bobby could be a liability in their quest. He'd go on when it was too dangerous, blinded by the desire to do what he thought was right.

And wind up condemning them all:

himself, Smoke, and the little girl, Mary-Ann.

'No, we stop,' she said. 'We make a camp, get there tomorrow.'

'You any idea what they could be doing to her? What men like that are capable of?'

'We don't know they still have her,' Smoke said evenly. 'And we don't know they'll be in Inferno either.'

She dismounted, patted her horse on the neck and fondled its ears. It had done a lot of travelling today, and she'd pushed it hard. Smoke had learned how important it was to be at one with your mount. There were no horses in North America until white men had arrived. But the natives of this country had soon learned to ride, and understood you needn't use a saddle to do so. She had ridden bareback when she was young, when she had been growing up as a taken girl. Some things from her stolen girlhood still lingered, like the colour of her hair, the soreness of her loss, and this also — a better thing, a fine thing

— the tending of horses.

Whispering in the dun's ear, she put it on a long tether. Already Smoke was undoing the clasps and buckles of the saddle. She would brush down the horse's flanks, no matter how tired she was herself. Some things you did, because some acts you had to honour. This was her way of doing right by her horse.

Behind her, she heard Bobby Lee cussing to himself but following her lead and dismounting.

At least he wasn't that far gone that he'd ride into Inferno alone and expect to come out of things all right.

★　★　★

Inferno. At the same time Danny was telling everyone in the show what he'd learned about the town, Bobby Lee told Smoke what he knew of the place.

They'd refrained from lighting a fire, snacked on cold ham and grainy biscuits. In the morning they'd risk a

112

small fire, to charge themselves with something warm to get them through the day. But at night, this close to town, it was too dangerous. Inferno kept to itself. If it knew people were close by and wasn't sure who they were, someone might come out for a look-see.

Part of Smoke liked the idea of eliminating its inhabitants one by one as they came out to investigate, but she didn't know she'd any real enemies there. Truth was exactly as she'd stated it to Bobby Lee earlier: they didn't know his niece was there, or that Jack Donovan and his men had come this way.

She thought about the tall man who'd come to the show to challenge her.

He hadn't been kidding about how fast he could draw. Smoke had seen fast shooters, thought herself one of them, but this guy Donovan was astonishing. Two guns out and levelled high in different directions in the time it'd taken her to get her gun out of its holster.

'Tell me again about this place we're going to,' she said to Bobby Lee.

Bobby Lee put down his knife and stopped whittling away at the piece of wood he'd picked out of the brush.

'Inferno was a crossroads town, only it wasn't a lucky crossroads town. Run down, gone to ruin, it had a bad reputation from the off. Maybe if Bradbury wasn't so close it might have prospered. But no, Bradbury's there, and Bradbury's fine, and that's where most people in these parts head out for.'

Smoke nodded. 'It's where Danny brought the show, heard there'd be good business there.'

'Zactly. Bet he's never even heard of Inferno.'

'What's it like?'

'Two streets intersecting, like any other crossroads town. But it never got any busier. And truth be told, where it is now, with all the towns getting bigger north and south of it, it's never gonna get any busier. It's all but abandoned. And the people who do live there, they're not the sort of people you'd want to keep as close acquaintances. It's all set for closing down,' Bobby Lee said. 'Yet somehow it never quite does.'

Smoke had seen abandoned towns before. They were hollow places, and the wind didn't seem to pass through them without slowing, or making mention of a few ghosts here and there. The Wendigo stalked such places, she thought — native beliefs instilled in her on top of her barely formed Christian upbringing before her parents had died. (*Murdered*, a voice whispered in the back of her head.)

'Sounds like the kind of place that draws bad men to it,' Smoke said.

She thought of the small town in which she'd lived with her ma and pa, remembered shutters clattering in the wind in deserted buildings, holes in the roofs of the houses and shacks. How the rain, cold and relentless during winter, could fall and make a swamp out of the dirt track they were calling the main street.

Bobby Lee nodded. 'It's nothing to recommend it.'

'And that's why you think Donovan's there,' Smoke said.

'There's something else,' he said. 'No one likes to talk about it, but it's there at the back of people's minds all the same. A girl like Mary-Ann, she's of interest to certain types. She's a pleasant-looking thing, just the right age, if you know what I'm saying.'

A cold strip of unease unrolled down Smoke's spine.

Bobby Lee said, 'There's certain kinds would pay to have a girl like Mary-Ann. And Inferno's the kind of place such men know they can get what they're after.'

Smoke had to work hard to control her voice, but she'd had to work hard an awful lot of times in her life to do that, when nightmares had come to her during the daylight hours, when she

116

was otherwise wide awake and not dreaming but still scared.

She said, 'Men like that don't deserve to live.'

Bobby had put away the wood at which he'd been whittling and had got his rifle across his lap as they spoke. He checked the breach and general condition of the stock and barrel.

'Amen to that,' he said.

10

In the end it was decided that me, Danny, Wheat and Clete were going to go after Smoke. The rest of the show would stay in Bradbury, with Buck keeping things under control. There were still some bottles of medicine left, and maybe like a muleback bakery the stock could be sold if taken around the houses. We couldn't take the women if there was likely to be shooting and we needed at least one man to stay. It might get tough. In fact, Danny had wanted me to stay too, and it'd taken a mighty long hour of arguing to get him to agree to me riding with him and the others.

Even then, Danny didn't really agree to me going so much as stop telling me I couldn't.

So when he, Wheat, Rayne, and Clete rounded up to set off, I nervously joined them. There weren't enough horses to spare to have one each if I was going, and Danny looked at me through slitted eyes. He snorted like he didn't have a decision to make and heeled his horse on. I looked up at Wheat who touched the brim of his hat, whistled, and followed Danny.

'Clete,' I said.

For a moment I thought he was going to say no too, but then maybe he thought on how I'd fought Spike when the two of them were wrestling.

He said, 'I guess so,' and reached out to me.

'Yes, sir!' I was eager to get up on the horse behind him, and I didn't care what some of the folks in town might think, a white boy riding behind a black man. This was Clete, and I respected and admired him.

We hadn't gotten far down Main Street when a buggy pulled by a dark horse with a splash of white between its eyes closed in on us. Danny brought us to a stop by raising his hand.

'What is it?' I said, making a hard job of seeing around Clete's bulk.

'Looks like that doctoring man you told us about,' he said.

'Doc Hannah,' I said. 'What's he want?'

'Ain't likely sure. If we listen up we might find out,' he said, a tad impatient with me.

'Doc,' Danny said as the buggy stopped. 'You here to talk us out of this, you're wasting your time.'

'No,' Doc Hannah said. 'I didn't think I'd be able to persuade you otherwise. You think too much of that girl of yours not to go. I understand that. And if it was someone close to me, I'd be doing the same as you are.'

'Then, much as it's appreciated, you not trying to talk us out of this, we ain't got the time to jaw here. We need to be on our way.'

'I understand that too. But I done some thinking about things,' the doc said, turning his head to look around the town. Evidently he didn't like what he saw there. 'Your boy Luther here, well yesterday he put us to shame in the sheriff's office. No matter what Virgil Cross and Findley Doon says about waiting for the marshal, what's true is that Bobby Lee Parker aside, ain't no one prepared to leave their easy life here to risk it against Jack Donovan and his men for one of our own, and a little girl at that. That's shameful, sir.'

Danny didn't say anything. Wheat Rayne studied his gloves, impatient to be getting on. Clete spoke up now, saying in that deep, warm-toned voice of his, 'You just apologizing for your town or offering us something here?'

The doc didn't look like he was used to being spoken at like that from a man who wasn't his own colour. Probably wasn't even used to it from a white man either, I reckoned. Some doctors can get right uppity about their position in society.

He looked at Danny when he answered and I felt Clete tense up at that.

'Your boy here's right,' he said — by 'boy' he was meaning Clete, I realized. 'I am here to offer something.'

'If you're saying you'll get a posse up with the marshal and we're welcome to join in,' Danny said, 'that ain't no use to us. We got one of our own to bring back now, and it looks like we might end up trying to get your missing girl too the way things are going.'

'Wasn't what I was about to offer,' the doc said.

'So what is it?'

'I'll come along with you. Ain't fired a gun in anger in a long time but I reckon I remember how to do it without shooting my foot off. Won't be a lot of use to you in any fighting, it's true, but I'll hang back, let you take the lead there. There's a chance someone's gonna wind up hurt, may need some help from me. Might be the difference between one of you making it back or not.'

Danny glanced at Wheat Rayne and

then at Clete, thinking on the doc's offer.

Wheat said, 'Reckon he could be useful if one of us does gets hurt, Danny. Plus there's something else,' he said, looking at the doc. 'You know where this town Inferno is? How to get us there?'

'Ain't the kind of place a man aims to travel to more than once,' the doc said. 'But I know where it is. Some of it ain't trailed from here, but I know the way. Saves the worry you might have of getting lost.'

'Then that settles it,' Danny said. 'You're in.'

That's how Doc Hannah came to join up with us. Way things went, it was a good job he did too.

★   ★   ★

Smoke looked out on Inferno for the first time that day. Bobby Lee had brought them out of a group of widely spaced pines near a good vantage point, high on top of a bluff. The sky was a blue tinted by verdigris and scalloped with high white clouds. Smoke knew how to read the signs, and understood there was a good chance rain would arrive tomorrow, but likely not today.

'I told you, place don't look much,' Bobby Lee said.

He spoke softly, as if afraid of being overheard even at this distance.

Smoke was scanning the town for signs of any familiar figures. Truth of it was though, that nothing much walked the dusty streets of the crossroads town. It was an 'X' on the map, with shanty buildings leaning against each other around the cross. If you shoved too hard on one, you could imagine the rest tumbling over as well. It looked dry as tinder.

'There's no one there,' she said. 'Looks like a ghost town.'

'No, there's people there,' Bobby Lee said. 'They just ain't busy.'

They lay side by side, keeping low to avoid any eyes the town might have.

Smoke had brought her rifle with her. She'd unsheathed it from her dun back in the trees and crept forward after Bobby Lee. His plaid shirt was dull enough not to cause too much of an attraction and shouldn't mark them out. Her own clothes were beige and dusty from the ride here. Force of habit had her click the hammer back on the rifle as she judged the distance to town. From here a shot was theoretically feasible, but even with her great skill, the chances of taking out any intended victim without letting a fusillade loose was slim.

That was, of course, assuming there was anything to shoot at.

'People in Inferno don't walk about much during the day,' Bobby Lee said, rolling onto his back. He lifted a canteen to his lips. 'Mostly it's a night town.'

'Can see why,' Smoke said. 'The less of it you see in good light, the happier you'll be.'

The windows, where they were still

intact, all looked dark. Either with drawn shades or because they let into rooms unused to anything but darkness.

'Want a drink?' Bobby Lee said, holding out the canteen.

'We're gonna have to go down there,' Smoke said.

Bobby didn't look so sure. The confidence — or drive — that had brought him this far faltered. 'Just walk in, without knowing where we're heading?'

Smoke would've shrugged but lying down like this made the gesture too awkward.

'We need to find out if Mary-Ann's there,' she said. 'And if she's not but Jack Donovan is, then we need to make him tell us what he's done with her. I'm not talking about strutting down Main Street and calling him out.'

Bobby Lee grunted. He rolled back on his belly, looked down at the lowly structures of the town.

'Whatever Donovan tells us, it may not be an answer you're comfortable with,' Smoke said.

Bobby Lee's fingers tightened around his rifle. Smoke saw the whites of his knuckles through the grit of his stained hands. 'No,' he said. 'I understand that.' Then he asked, 'When do we go down?'

'In a while,' Smoke said. 'Let's watch out a little longer, see what gives.'

Even now, knowing the worst of what could be happening to that little girl, she remembered Danny telling her this wasn't her fight or concern. Part of her knew Danny had been telling her the truth, that she shared no blood with the girl, and she hadn't made her a promise she was being held to. Something else was driving her. The same something that walked around inside her like a caged beast each time she caught a glimpse of her reflection and saw her hair, that brilliant white, and remembered that once it had been a deep chestnut colour just like her mommy's.

'We wait,' Smoke said, forcing her heart calm. 'We wait and we watch and we see what we see.'

It was an old way. It was an Indian way. She thought on the white of her hair, the red of her blood.

Minutes went by and stretched into half hours that become hours. They broke it in turns, so as not to cramp up or get so stiff they couldn't move. And eventually the reward for their vigilance arrived.

'There,' Bobby Lee hissed. 'Darn it, there!'

Smoke scrambled to the jut of rock at the edge of the bluff and followed the aim of his finger. There was movement in the town. Three — no, four! — figures, one of them considerably smaller than the others, moving between the buildings, slinking like shadows on the old walks. One of them was moving stiffly, and Smoke thought about the shot she'd fired at the voiceless one, Spike, back in Bradbury, how he'd jerked and nearly gone over, as her bullet had hit him.

Well, he was still alive, but for how long was another question.

'It's them,' Smoke said.

'Mary-Ann's there, she's alive.'

She had to dig her fingers into Bobby Lee's arm to prevent him getting up and running for his horse.

'Wait. Not yet. We gotta see where they go. By the time you got down there, they could be into another building or something. 'Less you're gonna shoot up the whole town, you'd get nowhere.'

Bobby was pumping to go, but he saw the sense in what Smoke was saying.

'Take it easy,' she said. 'The girl's alive, that's the important thing. Now let's watch on, see what they get up to.'

Jack Donovan and his friends didn't stay out in the open for long. Joad, the fatter one, was preventing the little girl from running away. Smoke understood that a young girl's spirit could be broken and left in a state not only of helplessness but of despair. But even though she was being herded on, the little girl wasn't making it easy for her captors.

They pushed at a door on a two storey building — not many of the structures in town rose above a single storey, so it wouldn't be hard to remember — but Smoke could see no identifying signs or clues as to what the building might be. A saloon or casino maybe, once upon a time, with rooms to rent upstairs. It was a pretty anonymous place.

Anyway, it's where Donovan, Joad and Spike were. More importantly, it was where Mary-Ann was too.

Smoke lay there staring, thinking without really thinking . . .

'You ever killed a man?' Bobby Lee said after some time elapsed.

Smoke blinked, surprised. 'Have you?'

'Rabbits. Squirrels. Once had to put a dog to rest. He was a good dog too. Hardest of all to say goodbye to. But an actual man . . . no. Though there have been some I've thought about killing in my time. Just never really got hot-headed enough to do it. I guess I thought on the consequences too much.'

'And now . . . ?' Smoke said. 'You feel any different about killing now?'

'Those men killed my sister and her husband. Took my niece with them and tried to make it look as how they'd flung her in a river. It hadn't been for Hank Peters jumping in after that bundle of rags, we'd be thinking she was dead too, washed away and drowned. And you know what? The more I think on it, more I reckon it might have been part of their plan the minute they got chased into my sister's house. You know what I'm saying?'

'They thought they could get some-thing for Mary-Ann,' Smoke said. 'All they had to do was get out of Bradbury and have folks think the girl was dead.'

'You never answered my question,' Bobby Lee said. 'Look at me and tell me. You ever killed a man?'

Smoke took her gaze away from the

building Jack Donovan and his crew had disappeared into and looked Bobby Lee Parker straight in the eye. She thought about her parents, her true parents, and how she'd seen them taken away and scalped and worse, thought of the Indian who'd done that and how, when she'd been older, and had endured all he could inflict on her, she had taken a knife to him in the night and cut him. Cut him first to stop him fighting back, cut him second to bring him some pain, cut him third to humiliate him and take away his means of ever hurting her again. Cut him last of all to kill him.

'Yes,' she said.

She saw that Bobby Lee believed her.

'And I'm about to kill some more,' she told him.

He believed that too.

11

Doc Hannah was good to his word and knew the way to Inferno. Once we were out of town, instead of keeping to the trail that Danny would have taken us along, he veered his buggy away west to the scrubland. Clete claimed he could see an old track here. But it must've fallen out of use years ago, because to my eyes we were stencilling in a new trail on the land.

It wasn't easy going without a clear path, but we managed.

We passed plane trees and alder trees and the odd thicket of varying density, from inside of which I thought I heard some free-roaming swine at one point, reminding me of how my life used to be before I signed up to Danny's Travelling Medicine and Jamboree Show. But mostly we followed open scrubland, rolling up and down gently curling rises and dips in the land and making good progress towards the distant hills, though because the doc was in his wagon we had to veer around rougher ground and that added to the time it was taking us.

The doc's buggy was a sprightly old thing, and rattled like a broken pocket watch on a cowboy with the ticks riding a bucking bronco, and he had to persuade his horse on with the whip now and again. But after a while I admitted to Clete that it might be better on my behind to ride with the doc rather than squat behind him on his horse, so I transferred over to ease my thighs and to reconnect my rear with some feeling.

The doc wasn't a conversationalist in the traditional sense. Maybe if he'd got Danny or Wheat as a companion it might have been different, but I think he took it upon himself to educate me somewhat, on account of what he called my tender years. Once he started talking, he was in the habit of talking *to* you, and not with you. I couldn't have sworn to the certainty of his facts, but he rightly seemed to know a lot about anything and everything in the world.

At length, I said to him, 'You know, Doc, if I had that much knowledge in my head, all the clever ideas of other men that you've picked up through what you're calling your leisure reading, then I'm not sure I'd have the room to do any thinking for myself.'

This didn't seem to faze the doc and he carried on educating me. At one point he mentioned some clever thinker and poet from years gone by, went by the name of Horace, and all I could add to the conversation was that we'd had a mule called Horace and he wasn't bright at all. In fact, he was pretty dumb. And cantankerous.

That shut the doc up for at least half a minute. Then he was at it all over again.

He plain wore me out with his highfalutin words, so that I was exhausted by the time we came to rest the animals. I was thinking of climbing behind Clete for the remainder of the journey and taking on the saddle sores.

Clete grinned at me when I dropped down off the wagon, and I reckon he must've known how I was feeling. I waved him off and looked to break out the meals Gretchen Fry had made up for us, kill the growls in my belly. My head was spinning and I'd have sworn I'd been riding with the doc for three days straight, with night forgetting to come out because its head was hurting as much as mine.

★   ★   ★

It was hard for either Bobby or Smoke to think up a plan that went much beyond sneak down into town, leave the horses tied up on the outskirts and hope no one discovered them, then sneak around the back of the buildings until they came to the one they'd seen Jack Donovan take Mary-Ann into and go bust her out.

The bit of the plan they hadn't liked to talk about was the bit where they'd be running for the horses with a little girl in their arms — while bullets filled the air around them like a swarm of bees.

As it went, things didn't happen that way.

★   ★   ★

'We're joining Langley's Pass around this spur,' Doc told us. The land had gotten trickier and there were exposed buffs of red rock rising here and there, a lot of pine forest and lonely trees in long grass twisted by the weather. 'That means we're back on what's left of the main trail between Bradbury and Inferno. Where we've come this far, ain't likely anyone would have cause to think twice on us. But now, there's only one way we'd likely be heading. We see anyone, then they're either on their way to Inferno or coming from there.'

'And if they've anything to do with

Inferno, they're trouble,' Wheat said.

'That about sums it up,' Doc said.

Wheat Rayne set his hat straight, put a hand to his guns. The stocks on his weapons were a pale bone colour. He wore a gun on each leg. Danny had just the one, a hefty Smith & Wesson. It threw out big bullets. If one of them hit you, you weren't getting up in a hurry. It was a good job, too, because Danny wasn't as good with a gun as he was with his sets of rope.

I checked to see what Clete was carrying. He didn't favour a handgun the way Wheat Rayne did. In the cavalry he'd shot with a rifle and it was the rifle he would turn to if there was any trouble today. He did have a handgun but lacked a belt. It was an old army issue Colt, black as coal and about as dusty at first glance, and he kept that in a saddlebag. I was empty-handed, and figured I'd be left to hold the horses or sit tight with the doc if it came to any action.

'All right. We ride on cautiously,'

Danny said. 'Keep your eyes open for any sign of Smoke and this guy Bobby Lee Parker. We got a description of him, Doc?' We had, and the doctor gave it to us. 'So that's who we're aiming not to shoot at,' Danny said. 'Hopefully, he's with Smoke, and she'll make sure he doesn't draw on us too.'

I looked up for the sun, trying to make a guess at the time. Afternoon was lengthening out and before long it would be evening. We'd done a lot of travelling today.

I wondered what Smoke was doing right now.

*　*　*

As it turned out, she was in the back of what had once been a bakery. There couldn't be much call for eating in Inferno, she was beginning to think, because as far as she could tell the few indications of life she had seen suggested the people here were as insubstantial as waifs, and as slow to

139

interact with you too; anyone saw you, they faded away into darker shadows and pretended not to notice you. Just a few steps behind her, treading softly now he'd removed his spurs, was Bobby Lee Parker.

Somewhere a door squealed and tapped its jamb in a breeze, an eerie knocking sound. The only things scuttling across the boardwalks and the cross streets were blown by the wind, and none of it was human. If you didn't know that Jack Donovan and his men were here holding onto Mary-Ann, or that behind the boarded windows pairs of gimlet eyes threaded with red veins looked out into the world, then you'd swear that not a person other than the two of them were here in Inferno.

Memories kept pushing to the fore in Smoke's mind. Memories of being a little girl and running around in the open. Something about the set of the buildings here, the way their shadows fell in stripes and wedges, lit up the crackle of the past intruding into her thoughts.

This wasn't right. She shook her head, had to concentrate on the now.

So how come she knew there was a thin alley ran between the side of the bakery and the building alongside it that had once been a general store?

A creeping sensation rose up Smoke's spine, speeding her heartbeat to a gallop so that she began to feel breathless, gripped by a panic she couldn't find the source of.

'You OK?' Bobby Lee whispered.

She put a hand to her chest, breathed out slow, as if to ease a sudden unexpected fright.

'I'm fine. We'll cut through the alley here, then we're in the shadows as we come out onto Main, a couple of buildings down from the joint Donovan went into.'

Bobby didn't ask how she knew the layout of town so well. She didn't know how she'd have answered him if he had. She squeezed on the grips of her pistols, both drawn now, tightened her eyes closed for a moment to shake off strange memories layering onto the present.

'All right,' she said. 'Let's do this.'

12

We heard the gunfire. It was faint, and flattened by distance, but there was a lot of it.

Because it was distant, we had to be sure we weren't fooling ourselves into thinking it was something else, like a crazy woodpecker taking on a whole forest in one go. To be sure, Danny raised an arm and drew us all to a halt. He looked to Wheat, who probably had better hearing than the rest of us put together. But with the wagon no longer rolling and the horses quiet, you didn't need to have Wheat's good senses to know it was gunfire we were listening to, however far away it might be.

Doc said, ''Tain't much more than a mile and a half off around that last stretch of trees by the bluff, a straight run to it. Inferno.'

In the still air of early evening, with

the sky a luminous yellow before the dark, and the moon hanging like a sickle blade in the first spots of starlight, we'd been looking to make camp and then perhaps scout ahead, see how the terrain lay. Maybe have Wheat walk into town if it looked like that was an option and see what he could learn. Now, that gunfire boded ill omens, and you didn't need Cara Treene's third eye to know nothing good could come of it.

'Smoke,' Danny said.

'Inferno's a lawless place,' Doc said. 'Could be it's just another dispute between drinking buddies gone wrong.'

'No. It's Smoke and Bobby Lee,' Wheat said. 'Most likely.'

Before Danny could tell us what to do next — and I likely admit I don't know what that might have been, but I guessed it would've involved heading off at a fast pace with guns drawn to confront something we had no idea about — the shooting went quiet.

'It's stopped,' I said.

'Hush up,' Clete told me.

Wheat tilted his head to one side, put his hat at the side of his head like it might amplify sounds and bounce them into his ear.

There was another shot, a single pop in the distance, and we all heard it; then, a few seconds later, another. There was nothing but an uneasy silence following on after that.

'Whatever's gone down there, sounds like it's over now,' the doc said. 'We may be too late already.'

'Yeah, and we might not,' Danny said, but we all of us knew that was bravado talking. He wasn't prepared to think that Smoke could be dead. None of us were. Except the doc, who appeared to have no real emotional ties to this posse and was here to do right by the honour of his town alone.

'Danny?' Wheat said.

'I'm thinking,' Danny said.

Wheat fastened his hat back on his head, made an observation we were all aware of.

'Getting dark,' he said. 'Not much more riding time left, even now we're back on a proper trail.'

'Yeah,' Danny said, like he was torn over things.

'What's it mean?' I whispered to Clete. The horse we were sharing had drifted away from the others slightly and Clete was letting it do as it pleased within reason. 'What are they saying?'

'That what's happened has happened and there might not be anything we can do about it, son.'

'But . . .'

'Danny's reckoning on how much of a risk it is for us to go on now or not.'

I couldn't believe Danny wasn't already high in his saddle, whipping out the last running in his horse. Smoke meant that much to him, I was sure. I was going to say as much, but Clete must've known that and he turned his shoulders so I nearly came off the back of his horse. He told me softly, 'You mind to keep your mouth closed and let Danny do his thinking now.'

146

I fumed quietly. If I'd had a horse of my own, by now I'd be racing to the west, looking to chase what was clear dusk before night fell.

'Doc,' Danny said eventually. 'You good to go on a little way?'

Doc Hannah nodded. He was tired. It had been a full day with a lot of riding and he'd been the one who'd got us here this quickly. But he was an older man, and the effort was stretching out his resources.

'I can do that. If we're careful,' he said, and it was impossible to miss that note of warning in his voice: *Don't go running us into Inferno like a blood-up posse*, he was saying.

'Then let's ride on,' Danny said. He sounded resigned to the worst. 'We do it quietly and we do it carefully. And we'll find what we find.'

'Without getting shot at,' the doc said.

'If we're lucky,' Danny admitted.

'Amen to that,' Clete said softly, but I knew he was concerned for Smoke.

He'd brought her up, hadn't he? She was as good as a daughter to him. And never mind she had the palest skin and the whitest hair I'd ever seen and Clete had the darkest skin and darkest eyes. He had some snow coming through in his hair, funnelling down his beard. Maybe they'd share that white hair someday, find it a source of conversation. I hoped so.

We set off into the dusk, hearts heavy, stomachs turning with ill bodings.

The lights of town showed as we reached the edge of a stand of trees. Lone pines edged out into the scrub beyond the thick of the woodland, below the wide bluff and steep incline to the top of the hills.

I say the lights of town, but that would be to suggest the place was lighted by kerosene lamps and there were candles and windows warm with life in them. Wasn't the case. The lights moving around town were torches, casting their flickering reach among the

crooked shadows and lopsided dark-
nesses of the old buildings.

Doc was right. Inferno wasn't much,
and in the coming dark it looked like it
was drawing a cloak around itself.

We sat our horses and watched the
moving lights cast an eerie glow about
the town.

'They're looking for someone,' Wheat
said.

'Meaning Smoke might still be alive,'
I said.

'Maybe.'

'But that has to be it, don't you see?
She and the guy she was with, this
Bobby Lee, they must have gotten in a
gunfight and now they're hunkered
down somewhere. Donovan and his
guys are looking for them.'

'Way I remember it,' Danny said,
'there was only three guys to worry
about. Donovan, Joad, and the one they
called Spike. Count the torches moving
around over there.'

There were ten, maybe twelve or
more of them.

'I don't understand,' I said.

'Means whatever's happened, it's involved more than just Smoke and Donovan's crew,' Wheat said.

'Anyone in Inferno,' Clete said to the doc, 'they'd side with Donovan?'

'Be sure to,' Doc said, speaking into the air and not allowing Clete the satisfaction of his gaze landing on him.

We'd drawn to a halt before we were visible from town. I'd jumped down off the back of Clete's horse, and at his insistence, climbed aboard the doc's buggy. My braces had slipped off my shoulders, and I hoisted them back up and pulled my undershorts from the crack of my behind, where sweat had rolled off my back like a river looking for a cave to the sea. Clete called me back to him now.

'Luther.'

'Yes, sir?'

'Here. You got an idea what to do with this?'

He had reached into his saddlebag

and pulled out his old Colt pistol. It wasn't as elegant a weapon as the ones Wheat and Danny carried; its lines were boxy and clumsy, and the hammer had to be pulled back manually before you could squeeze the trigger.

But as I took it from Clete, I felt a mite better than I had a moment ago, standing in the uncertain light of dusk with nothing but my bare fists to ward off any threat that might be thrown at me.

'It's heavy,' I said and immediately felt like a fool.

'Tends to kick like a mule when you fire it,' Clete said. 'But you point it and don't be scared to shoot if you have to. Might not hit anything, but it could distract someone aiming to shoot you. And you take any advantage you can in that situation, you hear?'

I did. I held onto the gun as I looked into the falling night and watched the lights move about Inferno, blurring detail in crimson flickers along the streets. I thought of Smoke and the

151

man who was helping her, and I thought of the little girl who'd been too long in the hands of men who were wicked to the bone. I knew then that I wouldn't falter when it came to putting a bullet into such a creature. In a sense, those men represented the bad fate that had touched my parents. A remorseless thing without pity or compassion. Inhuman.

For it was as Clete had tried to tell me: some men are true and good, and though they may fail to live up to the goodness expected of them by the Lord, they tried their best. And then there were other men who were not really men at all, but animals in the clothes of men, wearing a face and skin the way a good man will wear a Stetson and a vest and decent rawhide clothes. Except underneath, they were something else altogether.

'Hey now,' Wheat said.

'What is it?' Danny said.

'Something coming,' Wheat hissed, and slid off his mount. 'Let's lead the horses out of sight. Get that trap over there, Doc.'

Doc did so, and I can't say it didn't make a sound, but he clucked his horse on gently. The buggy was the quietest it had been all day, with only a little squeak coming out of it here and there. Doc didn't try his luck. He just steered into a wide space on the flattest ground between some upright trees and when it looked like the dark had swallowed all it could of him, he came to a stop.

Wheat Rayne and Danny pulled their horses by the bridle reins, and Clete, still riding, lay low on his horse and spoke softly into her ear as he edged her into the tree line.

I was left standing out in the open, the old army Colt in my hand, and for a moment I dared myself to stay out there before I sank into a crouch and made my way to the nearest of the pines. It didn't afford enough cover to make me invisible by daylight, but in the half-light of dusk, I figured I was safe enough.

And then I heard it.

Sure as his word, Wheat had been right. Something was coming this way, and it didn't sound to be in good health. It was gasping with heavy breaths, bigger than a man, and I latched my sight onto it, saw a misshapen monstrosity lurching along the road out of Inferno.

Whatever it was, it was moaning and chattering on its breath, little misshapen prayers and cusses combined.

Wasn't until it was up close that I saw it for what it was. A man, pained with the burden of what he was carrying, sobbing as he came.

My heart all but shook out any sense I had remaining, for fear was running wild in me then. If I'd had to, I don't know that I could have kept my gun level, my hand was shaking so.

Danny stepped out of concealment, hissed at the man, 'Hey.'

The man fell to his knees, and now the sobs came clear and the anguish lit his voice with a sound that was terrible to hear.

'Aww, no . . . Aw no. Please don't, please don't, we was only trying to take back what was stolen from us. We was only trying to get a little girl back . . . '

The curled blade of the moon showed me what he let fall to the ground as he himself collapsed to his knees.

'Smoke!'

I rushed forward. She wasn't moving. She was dead weight on his back, and now she was a lifeless sack of blood and bones beside him.

13

'She ain't breathing,' Doc said.

'She's dead?' Danny said. His voice, so unlike the showman I knew, was weak and trembling and I feared he might fall down where he stood.

'Not been gone long, though,' the doc said. 'She's warm.' He turned Smoke on her back, put her head carefully still, parted her lips. He put his fingers in her mouth, fished around inside, squinting till he pulled on something. 'Got her tongue clear,' he said, but it sounded as if he was talking to himself as much to us. 'Right, the next part.'

The next thing he did was a mite obscene on a dead person, especially if you didn't know her. He pressed his mouth up against hers and looked to be giving her a kiss to try to make her breathe, only it wasn't like a kiss in a fairy tale from some handsome prince (not only did the kiss fail on that score, but the doc wasn't handsome except perhaps to a turtle, which he sort of resembled on the facial features front).

For a moment I wondered if he'd lost his mind.

After he'd done pushing his lips up on her, he pumped at Smoke's chest with his hands, counting softly as he went, then kissing her again in that obscene fashion.

'What's he doing?' I said.

The doc answered when he came up for air. He sounded like he was running from one sea to the other without a pause. 'Breathing for her. Trying to get her heart going. Heard about this but never actually tried it.' His hat came off but he didn't stop. He flipped between puffing into her mouth and then going like a jackrabbit on her chest. 'Harder work than I thought it'd be.'

'She's dead,' Danny said again, and this time he did sink to the ground, though how much of that was due to the doc's strange approach to medical matters and how much sheer shock and horror, I didn't know.

We stood around, those of us still able to stand, and watched in silence. The doc's strength was petering out; he was tiring quickly.

Clete sank to his haunches beside the doc. 'What can I do?' he said.

The doc fell back exhausted. He couldn't go on. He waved at Smoke, said, 'Hands over her heart, one on top of the other, then keep pressing and lifting, but not so hard you snap her ribs.'

Even in the poor light, sweat swamping the doc's forehead was clear to see. He inhaled deeply, trying to catch his own breath.

'Count it out,' he told Clete, evidently no longer caring he was working alongside a man of colour. 'One, two, three, four, one, two, three, four . . . '

Clete did as he was instructed. 'The breathing. What do I do with the breathing? Come on, Doc. Now ain't the time,' Clete said, seeing the doc's distaste at the thought of Clete pressing his lips to Smoke's.

'Take a breath, squeeze her nose shut, and then blow into her mouth,' the doc said and turned away, as if he couldn't stomach the sight.

Clete did as he was told, then went back to pumping Smoke's chest.

And then some sort of miracle occurred out in that timeless zone between dusk and dark, when the cut of the moon and the first stars shone brighter by the second.

Smoke coughed, and seemed to lurch from her middle, her arms flailing, her legs kicking with a feebleness a newborn might manage. Clete quit at her chest, hands hovering over her, unsure if he should carry on or not.

The doc said, 'Well shoot, it does work. I never thought it would. Fancy that.'

★ ★ ★

Clete and Danny lifted her into the flatbed at the back of the doc's small buggy. A full-grown man couldn't be laid out in there, but Smoke almost fit. Her feet hung off the edge and I noticed one of her boots had come off. We tried to make her comfortable. I'd unrolled a blanket. Danny had removed his coat and scrunched it up for her to use as a pillow.

She was breathing but was in a confused state, seemed unsure of where she was and who we were.

'I need some light so I can examine her. She get shot or something?' the doc said, calling over to Bobby Lee, who was still laid out on the trail, his own exhaustion playing hard on him.

When Bobby Lee didn't answer, Doc told us to fetch him over, make him talk.

I ran over and Clete lumbered behind me. Between us we hoisted Bobby Lee to the buggy. Wheat was keeping a watch on Inferno, the stock of his rifle resting on a thigh, while Danny

160

set a kerosene lamp going in the back of the buggy. As well as the lamp there was a good number of supplies, food and medical. I reckoned the doc must have been fixing for a long campaign out here.

'Bobby Lee, you know me,' the doc said, holding Bobby Lee's face so he could speak straight at him. 'It's Doc, Doc Hannah. I treated you for that foot rot you came down with when you were nothing but a little one, you remember? And that time you got buckshot in your rear, I spent an afternoon cleaning up the wounds. Helped your Elisabeth all I could as well. You remember?'

Something like recognition swam through whatever fever had taken Bobby Lee and he looked at the doc, squinting.

'Doc, hey yeah, Doc Hannah. Only you didn't save Lillybeth, she's gone. My Lillybeth's gone.'

'Hold up now, don't go soft on me,' Doc said. 'We don't got the time for that. You need to tell me what happened to the girl here.'

Bobby Lee looked at Smoke, took a moment to think on who she was, and then got what the doc was asking.

'We went in for Mary-Ann,' he said. 'Saw where they'd taken her. Got the drop on them, thought it was gonna be easy. Only as we were about to go in a couple of wagons rolled into town, a lot of men on horses too. We weren't sure what was happening, so we ducked back down, listened in on what turned out to be a deal Jack Donovan had tried to get up and running. Then we got spotted. Suddenly we were in a crossfire, shooting just to stay safe. Smoke tried to get the girl out anyway, but part of the building came apart. Whole place is falling to pieces, the walls are so rotted you could walk right through them. Makes you wonder how anyone could live there. Anyway, Smoke got banged up pretty good under a lot of timber, hurt her head. I dragged her out, shooting all the while. I thought she was okay though, and we lasted out, trading shots till the sun went down, then there was more shooting and Smoke came on all woozy, like the wall falling in on her had only just caught up with her. She talked funny for a while, said as how she needed to go to sleep. Then when it was dark enough, I shot at some guys, and got us out of there.'

Doc nodded and went to sit with Smoke.

'Who were the men?' I said.

Bobby Lee looked at me, confused. 'Ain't you kinda young to be out here?'

'Who were they?' Clete said.

'I don't know. The ones in the carriages, they wore expensive suits. The riders with them looked like hired guns. They were all mean. Smoke and me, we heard some of why they were there. That's why we tried to get Mary-Ann out even though they were bad odds. Donovan was looking to sell the girl. Looked like there was gonna be an auction between these guys.'

Clete looked at me, and I knew what he was thinking. He was thinking of men who were not men, who wore the shape of men but were something far worse.

'We got to go save her,' I said. 'Don't we, Clete?'

Clete rubbed on his chin. The silver bristles on his jaw lighted up with a touch of the moon's shine.

'Smoke was our concern,' he said. 'That's who we came for.'

'Yeah, but Clete . . . you heard what the man said. What they're gonna sell that girl for, it ain't so she can work as a maid on a big old ranch somewhere.'

'World's a hard place,' Clete said. 'But we got Smoke back, that's what we gotta think on.'

'You rescued a girl before, Clete. Where's that man now?'

Before the last word had left my lips, Clete swung on me. I got whipped a good one across the mouth and a sky full of stars spun above me, it and the ground swapped places and I wasn't sure which was which, except I was lying on one of them.

Fingering the side of my face where Clete had hit me, I watched him walk away, a man not at all happy with himself and the choice he had to make. What was worse was that I knew Danny would think the same way. Wheat Rayne would side whichever way Danny's argument fell. And the doc was only here to honour the town's pride.

I got up on my feet. Bobby Lee was shaking now. He sank down and it was only then that I realized that he'd blood on his back. And if it wasn't from carrying Smoke, the only place it could've come from . . .

'Doc! Hey, Doc! Bobby Lee's been shot.'

14

'The Indians have a saying,' Smoke told us. Her voice was husky, as if it was still coming back to life. 'You are not a brave until you have travelled beyond this world into the next and returned.'

'I think you've been brave enough for anyone,' I said. My lips were swollen from Clete's whipping, and talking hurt me, but I felt that needed saying.

Smoke nodded. It pained her to do so. She was sore from having half a building collapse on her. She put a hand on my thigh, and I'll admit a flush of heat spread through me at her touch. 'I've returned from the dead twice now,' she said. 'Once when I was a little girl, and now here. And both times that death occurred to me in Inferno.'

Danny raised his eyebrows at her questioningly.

'I was born there,' she said. 'I didn't

recognize it at first. When me and Bobby got there and I looked out at it from up on the bluff over there, something stirred in the back of my mind. I knew the layout of the town, had these memories coming back to me. They were even stronger when me and Bobby Lee prowled around the back of the buildings. That's why we weren't caught — because I knew all the places kids would hide when they were playing games. Places a grown-up wouldn't think to look. And I knew this because it's where I grew up, before Ma and Pa were killed and I was taken away.'

'I thought your pa was a cowboy, drove cattle,' Clete said. He wouldn't look at me, but I didn't think he was still angry at me; he was upset with himself for striking out at me like he had. 'That's what you told me.'

'That's what I always imagined he was, what I wanted him to be. Truth is I have no real memories of him. So maybe he wasn't. Maybe he was something else,' Smoke said. 'Maybe he was about what Jack Donovan and his men are about. Maybe I was lucky I was taken by the Indians.'

If that was the best luck you could hope for, I didn't much fancy sharing in it.

The doc walked over. He'd his shirtsleeves rolled up, was cleaning off his hands on a rag. Behind him, the kerosene lamp flickered like a firebug. 'He'll live,' he said. 'But he won't be flexing that back without a twinge for a good few years to come. Way I reckon it, he'll be able to forecast snow a month in advance, the way his bones will hurt. Bullet was pretty close to his spine. He did well to get you out, ma'am.'

'He's a good man,' Smoke said.

'Reckon we owe him for that at least,' I said. 'Bringing Smoke out.'

Danny looked into the small fire we sat around. He'd got it going but used wood that smoked heavily. There weren't many flames. But it was a warm fire. You just had to keep out the path of that smoke if it chose to turn and twist. No one would see it from Inferno; the flames weren't bright enough, and Danny had set the fire so the trees hid it. Still, we were being careful, and Wheat and I swapped turns at keeping an eye out on the road to town to make sure no one was coming out here after Smoke and Bobby.

'Luther's right,' Smoke said.

Clete said, 'No, by saving you Bobby Lee only returned the favour you was doing him by going after the girl in the first place. You don't owe him a thing. Don't owe that little girl anything either.'

'You didn't owe me anything, Clete, but you took me away from that Indian settlement, raised me. And you raised me to do right by people. You call walking away from that little girl the right thing to do? Because I don't. And come first light, I'm going back to Inferno.'

'I could stop you,' Clete said.

'But you know better than to do that,' she said and stood up. She was slow to move, but the doc had assured us the only real problem she had was from a bad blow to the head. She'd a bump there like an egg but the skin wasn't broken. She needed rest, time to rebuild her strength. But she wasn't going to allow herself that.

'I'll come with you, Smoke,' I said. 'If these ain't up to it, I am.'

'Looks like the boy's more of a man than the rest of you,' she said.

When no one said anything, she spat on the fire, and I thought there might've been some blood mixed in with her spittle. It was dark enough for that.

'Dunno why, but it tastes like I've been kissing a skunk's butt,' she said as she limped to the saddles, found a blanket, and fumbled herself out a bed for the night.

★ ★ ★

I didn't sleep much. Danny and Wheat talked some; I heard that though not the actual words of their conversation. Clete was silent, a brooding presence like a bear in the middle of a church. Everyone stayed clear of him, most especially the doc, who was keeping an eye on Bobby Lee and now and again checking on Smoke.

But I did close my eyes, and somewhere between night and morning I caught some sleep. It was the sound of movement that woke me.

Smoke was up, preparing to ride in and try to rescue the girl. The fire had been left to go out, was a bundle of ruby embers. The smoke that wouldn't be seen during dark would give up our presence in a minute with daylight.

A pearly greyness filled my eyes. False dawn creeping in, a stain in the sky. It looked like an ill day to come.

I'd walked out a ways on the trail to Inferno last night, during one of the times I was keeping watch, and I'd found Smoke's missing boot. I could've turned back with it straight away, but I didn't, I kept going toward town, daring myself a little closer till I got too scared to go on. It was odd to think Smoke had been born and lived there, till the Indians had come in on a raid and taken her away. According to the doc, Inferno had always had a bad reputation. It wouldn't have been the first town built on whoring and drinking, but for some reason those who were most keenly drawn to Inferno were especially cruel and somehow that seemed to stain the town, twist its buildings and sour the land on which it was built. Could Smoke really have come from people like that?

I climbed out of my blanket, noting a faint dew had settled and a light dampness hung in the air. It'd get chased off as the day got properly underway.

Smoke didn't say anything as I got ready. And I couldn't think of anything to say to her. It was something we did wordlessly, like we knew we were fighting a hopeless cause and going against the wishes of those who cared for us most. It was almost as if we were the ones who should be shamed and not the others.

The doc was awake, smoking a thin cigar. He watched us. He didn't talk. I got the feeling he might have helped Smoke get dressed this morning, maybe tried to dissuade her from her course of action. She was moving stiffly and hadn't the full range of her limbs yet. He was on his buggy, a blanket around his shoulders as the mist seeped into the trees and Bobby Lee snorted in his sleep in the flatbed, wrapped in as many blankets as we could spare.

I snapped my braces on tight so my breeches wouldn't fall down at an inopportune moment, and gripped the gun Clete had given me last night. It had five bullets in it. Clete hadn't given me any spares. He wasn't asleep, I knew that, but his back was turned to us on purpose, and I didn't like to ask if he'd got any more. Five was probably more than I'd get chance to fire off anyway.

'You ready?' Smoke said to me. She

didn't look her best, but in the early light she could've been an angel all the same, one that was ready to start a shoot out. She was down to one pistol herself, but her gunbelt was more than half full with bullets. She wouldn't run short.

'I reckon so,' I said.

So with my guts churning ready to bring up the last food I'd eaten, we set off on foot for Inferno.

15

We'd been walking about five minutes
and the town was growing clearer to my
eyes by the second. The more I saw of
it, the less I liked it. It truly looked like
one of those ghost towns parents tell
their kids about to give them a fright.
Its windows were flat and lifeless, yet it
felt like they were watching your every
step. The buildings were not so much
upright as crooked and canted, leaning
one way and the next, as if crippled and
contorted with sickness.

'We just gonna walk right in?' I said.
'Not gonna skirt around and try sneak
up on them?'

Smoke stopped in the middle of the
trail. She'd taken one of Wheat's
cigarettes and had sucked it down to its
end. She threw it to one side now,
breathed out a visible blue cloud.

'That gun Clete gave you, Luther,

can I take a look at it?'

I handed it to her. I'd been carrying it in alternate hands on account of how heavy it was. I expected Smoke might need two hands to raise it. But she was stronger than I thought. She looked the gun over, broke its chamber open.

'There's five bullets in there,' I said, as if she couldn't see as much.

She snapped the chamber closed, forced the gun in her spare holster, glared at Inferno like she was eyeing up the opposition in a feud and just about to start the fight.

'Hey,' I said. 'Smoke.'

'Go back to Danny, Luther,' Smoke said. 'Go back there now. This isn't your fight. You're too young for this.'

'I'm only a bit younger than you.'

When Smoke looked at me then, I saw the lie in that truth. She might only have a few more years on her clock, but she'd travelled in those years, racked up experiences I couldn't even begin to imagine.

'Are you?' she said.

I shrugged, feeling suddenly small and helpless.

'Come here,' she said, not unkindly.

I was only a couple of steps from her, and wasn't sure what she wanted, but I moved closer. She leaned in and at first I ducked back. She hushed me and told me to stay still. Then she kissed me.

It wasn't what I expected. Clete had talked about taking me to a whore house soon, easing up the bubble building in me, and I didn't know if I'd been looking forward to that or not. Smoke kissed me aggressively, like she was assaulting me. Her tongue forced itself in on my mouth, and she seemed to be eating me up as much as anything else.

All the same, something in me liked it and when she broke off and released me I felt like she'd filled me with a fire that wanted to blaze all the brighter.

'Smoke?' I said, shaking my head dumbly.

Maybe part of me was hoping she'd tell me that she loved me and all the rest of that stuff you hear folks talking about when they turn romantic. But it didn't happen.

'Go back to Danny and Clete,' she said. 'Go live some life before you give up what you have, Luther. You're a good boy. Stay that way. And if this doesn't work out right, think of me sometimes, OK?'

With that, she left me standing there hot and empty-handed, with my head all a-whirl. I felt as if I'd grown wings and lifted up in the air, only to have them snatched away from me so I fell tumbling to earth, something vital and unexpected lost and gone.

★ ★ ★

I watched Smoke walk the rest of the way into town. It was like no one was up yet, as if Inferno was a creature that rose as one, a beast of the night, and it didn't think anyone would be foolish enough to go in at it alone and disturb its sleep.

Maybe that's why Smoke got as far as she did. Maybe that's why no one challenged her. Or I was being a romantic fool, and it was simply the case that last night there'd been a lot of carousing and stuff after a long time hunting down Smoke and Bobby Lee, and the gunmen and whatever whores there were in town were exhausted from their antics.

I stayed where I was, watched Smoke get eaten up by the town and then disappear at the crossroads, her favoured gun drawn, the one she'd taken from me still holstered.

Took a while for some sort of thinking to start working in my head again. I touched my lips, imagined I could still taste Smoke and wondered what I should do.

Without a gun I was no use to her. But the truth of it was that she didn't think I'd be much use to her with a gun either. Making a strange logic out of this, I shook my head and called myself a darned fool for letting her go on alone, and started to run after her.

As I ran it sounded like my feet were horses' hoofs and I was pounding my way to Inferno as part of a cavalry charge.

It was only when Danny and Wheat Rayne rode by that I realized I hadn't been making that sound in my imagination. And then, real quickly, another horse was beside me, a hand grabbed the back of my shirt, and I was propelled into the air by Clete, my legs pulled up after me as if my braces were holding them on.

'Grab hold behind me,' Clete called and I did just that, scrambling around like one of those monkeys I'd seen in some of our rival travelling shows. 'Don't you lose your grip now, this is hard travelling.'

It was. But it was exhilarating travelling too.

For a moment I near all but forgot that we were racing into danger. My heart soared because we were going after Smoke, were going to kick Jack

Donovan's plans to hell and grab back that little girl before he sold her to some man with a seriously skewed sense of right and wrong.

I'd been kissed by a beautiful girl and now I was riding into battle for her.

It felt righteous.

* * *

We rode into Inferno. Danny and Wheat were in the lead, and they broke down to a slow canter, a pistol each out, rifles sheathed but ready for use. Behind Clete, gripping onto him, I eyed the buildings on either side of the street with suspicion, half expecting a creaky old door to open and a gunman to appear.

But Inferno looked worse than deserted. It looked dead. It looked like whatever walked its streets did so without breath or heartbeat. If there was a living to be made here, then it was a living made of dust and cobwebs; it was painful, cruel, and held no pity for human life. The scent of decay and dry-rot hung in the air. I could understand how a wall had fallen on Smoke in all the fighting yesterday.

Doc Hannah had told us that some folks still lived here and Smoke had allowed she'd glimpsed people in the buildings. But if they were here, then I believed they were thin, like sticks wearing rags, and kept so well hidden only someone born in shadows might see them clearly. I thought I caught sight of movement every now and again, but only at the edge of my eye. When I focused in on that particular spot, there wasn't nothing there. Or else what had been there was gone, as if it shied away from the gaze of someone who lived his life out in the open like it shied away from sunlight.

Clete had his rifle across the pommel of the saddle, and he said on a breath, 'Watch out for anything, Luther, and get ready to hop off and run, if you need to. You shoot like I told you to if you have to.'

'Yes, sir,' I said, figuring it was a little late to admit to not having his pistol any more.

Before we got to the crossroads, I heard someone call, and it took me a moment to recognize Smoke's voice. It wasn't the clear chime I knew from the jamboree show. It had a hoarseness to it, still hadn't fully recovered from her passage from this world to the other and back.

Danny raised an arm and all three horses came to a stop as we listened to Smoke.

'Hey in the town!' she shouted. 'Jack Donovan! Jack Donovan! Where are you, Donovan?'

Smoke was calling him out.

'What'll we do?' I whispered.

'Get off,' Clete said. 'Run on over there.'

I slid off the horse and ran in front of Danny and Wheat's rides, going to a building standing on the corner of the crossroads. It might've been a store one time, but now just looked like a mausoleum left to rot. With some care due to the condition of the planking, I passed across the boardwalk and put my head around till I could see Smoke. Behind me, I was aware of Danny and Wheat edging their horses into the middle of the intersection, just waiting there. When I looked for Clete, I didn't see him, but he'd pulled his horse over to a hitching post and tied it off. I'd be surprised if the post stopped the horse from going if it wanted to, for it looked as rotten and ready to bust as the rest of Inferno. But I guess that wasn't the point.

'Jack Donovan!' Smoke called again.

Her hair shone now as the sun rose fully, looked whiter than anything I'd ever seen.

A door opened down the street and a man dressed all in black came out onto the porch. It wasn't Jack Donovan. He wore a gunbelt but his hands were about the making of a cigarette. He lit up and tossed the match aside, walked into the middle of the street. I couldn't figure what was happening.

Smoke said, 'I got no argument with you. It's Donovan I'm here for.'

The guy didn't say anything. His head was down as he walked up the middle of the street. I could hear the spurs on his boots jangling as he came. About twenty feet from Smoke he stopped and lifted his head.

Still didn't say anything.

Then he spat out his cigarette and went for his gun.

Smoke beat him. She drew and fanned down once on the hammer of her pistol. Shot him centre of the chest, catapulting him backwards. He sprawled on the floor, twitched for a while like he might be missing the hat that'd come off his head and dropped right where he'd been standing. A moment later he went still.

I breathed again, saw that his gun hadn't even cleared his holster before Smoke had hit him.

Smoke's shoulders lifted and fell, and I realized she must be breathing quickly, high on a blood rush at this point. I didn't know then about her history, that this wasn't the first man she'd killed. I should've figured out from what Bobby Lee had said that there'd been fellows who hadn't taken too lightly to Smoke's bullets hitting them last night. Maybe this guy was the partner of someone she or Bobby had killed yesterday and he had wanted his chance at revenge.

Well, the way it had gone, it didn't work out for him.

A moment or two of silence passed, and Smoke's shoulders stopped rising and falling. She took a steadying breath and I edged closer to her, moving along the covered walk in small steps, as close to the walls and dust-filmed windows of the building as I could, aiming to stay invisible by staying in the shadows and edging behind barrels and the old boxes left on the boards.

'Jack Donovan!' she cried, and this time she really did cry out, bringing his

186

name up from deep inside, so that it hurt to hear it.

'I hear you,' Donovan said, and he wasn't ten feet away from me.

Smoke spun around. She still had her gun in her hand and had it aimed now. Donovan was leaning in an open doorway of one of the two-storey buildings in town. There weren't many of them by my counting, three at most. Inferno was a low-rise town. Wasn't even a church bell-tower visible. His hands were empty but he wore his gunbelt; he was tooled up.

'Don't shoot just yet,' Donovan said. 'Wouldn't be fair. You being the fastest gun in the West and already having your weapon out in the open.'

'Where's the girl?'

'Well, now,' Donovan said, breaking into a smile. 'I don't rightly see what concern that is of yours.'

'I'm taking her with me,' Smoke said.

'Something about you that's awful familiar, girl,' he said with a lecherous smile. 'Knew it the first time I saw you,

187

only I couldn't place it.'

'You don't know me,' Smoke said, though her voice faltered and I could hear the uncertainty there.

'Just shoot him, Smoke,' I called.

Donovan glanced at me and dismissed me in a huff of breath when he saw I wasn't armed. He'd already spotted Wheat and Danny out in the middle of the intersection, where they'd heeled their horses. I figured Clete was the only one of us he didn't know about, unless someone had watched us ride into town.

'Shoot him,' I cried again.

Smoke nearly did as I told her. I could see her biting on that trigger. Another half an ounce of pressure would have blown Jack Donovan away to nothing. But she didn't. What he'd said had got to her.

Donovan hitched a thumb in his gunbelt. 'Been racking my brains, asking myself, now why do I know that girl?' He stepped off the boardwalk, out into the street. He touched two fingers to his hat in salute to Danny and Wheat down the road, but kept going, putting himself the same distance the man in black had done from Smoke, only on the other side of her now, so that he had Danny and Wheat to his back.

'Hope your friend isn't gonna pull his lasso trick on me again. That'd be mighty unfair.'

'He won't touch you,' Smoke said.

'That a promise?' When Smoke didn't reply, Donovan grinned. 'That's OK. Truth is, I got some people here myself. Hey Joad, Spike, come on out. Bring out the others, yeah.'

They were further down the street, both carrying Winchesters, and they came out of the shadows behind Smoke. They paid the dead man on the hard-pack no heed. Smoke cast a glance over her shoulder, but only a quick one, because she didn't want to take her eyes off Donovan. Four other men forced themselves onto the walks, all armed. Two behind Smoke, two between Donovan, Danny and Wheat. Bad odds.

189

'Was the hair that fooled me,' Jack Donovan said when the situation was clear. 'Little girl I remember, lived here in town, she had the richest chestnut hair you'd ever seen. Nose just like yours, and cute as a rainbow.'

'No,' Smoke said so quietly I had to read her lips.

'Cindy Winters, that was her name. Her pa rode with me.'

'No,' Smoke said more firmly. 'No, he didn't.'

'Oh, I think you'll find he did. Until there was this misunderstanding and things got a bit heated. Would've been interesting to see how the argument panned out. Only it was interrupted by some Indian trouble. Suppose the outcome was the same as it would've been anyway, with your pa dead and me alive and you taken off somewhere. That the reason you're here, to stop something like what happened to you happening to this little girl?'

When Smoke didn't say anything, Donovan shook his head. 'Like your pa, too sentimental. Sorry the Indians took you. You'd have brought us a pretty penny, make no mistake.'

'No!' Smoke cried and put her hands to her head, her free hand and her gunhand.

I saw what was going to happen before anyone else, and shouted, 'He's gonna draw!'

Jack Donovan was as fast as before, and he wasn't hampered by Danny Roden's lasso this time. His hand moved like it was oiled to his pistol and he'd drawn and fired before I'd finished shouting.

Smoke ducked to her left but the bullet caught her high all the same, nicking her right shoulder, and her pistol flew from her hand. She spun around, twirling and falling to land on her knees before lying flat out.

I threw a length of wood I snatched out of the rotting boardwalk at Jack Donovan, and it only just fell short, bouncing on its end. At least it distracted him enough to miss Smoke with his second shot.

By now Danny and Wheat had their guns up and were firing. First off they went for Donovan but they had to be careful in their shooting or they might hit Smoke. Second round they had to put to the gunhands who'd slunk out onto the boardwalks when Donovan had called them out.

While they were doing that, Jack Donovan spun on a heel and put a bullet in the horse that Wheat was riding. Wheat's mount buckled out underneath him, its front legs collapsing just before the back ones, pitching him forward as the horse's tail fanned up in the air before the whole creature lay still as a stone. I hurled an iron weight that lay on top of the barrel nearest me at Jack Donovan, and this clipped him on the shoulder just as he ducked the returning fire from Danny's big weapon. I reckon my iron did some good, because when Donovan fired at Danny he missed, which was the second shot of his I'd seen go astray today.

Now Joad and Spike and the other

gunhands down that end of the street joined in the shooting, aiming at Danny and Wheat. So far no one had a mind to fire in my direction. I heard other shots sounding too, but they weren't coming from any visible source. I figured that had to be Clete letting go with his rifle. Smoke was crawling to the side of the street, wounded but alive.

I ducked into the building Jack Donovan had come out of, just as he rained some shots at me. They hit the wood not an inch after my departing behind, and I swear I heard one whiz by my ear as if it were an angry bee out to teach me not to steal its honey.

Outside, the shooting went on, but in here it wasn't much quieter. The sounds of a rifle being fired came from upstairs, and I heard Clete shouting as he went from room to room, kicking in doors and likely picking off more of the gunmen Bobby Lee had told us about. I got my bearings, looking around. This place might have been a casino in its past, for it had the makings of one. There was a dusty old bar, card tables with green baize set on them and a bigger table with a roulette wheel. Stools and chairs were scattered around. All stood darkly gathering the debris of the ages. On one wall was the frame where a mirror had hung before the glass got shattered.

I knew I ought to see if I could help Clete, but without a weapon I didn't stand much hope. I wondered why my ear stung so, and when I put my hand to it I found it came away bloodied. Jack Donovan hadn't missed me entirely then.

Two men appeared at the top of the stairs, both overweight and soft. They weren't wearing gunbelts, but each carried a pistol. Between them was a little girl.

'Mary-Ann,' I said before I realized I'd have been best hushing my big mouth and sneaking up on them if I was going to rescue her.

They stumbled to a halt a few steps from the bottom of the stairs. One levelled his gun at me, the other turned with real fear in his eyes to what was occurring upstairs, where the gunfire hadn't relented and screams, male and female, rose in intensity.

'Who're you?' the one aiming the gun at me said.

'Luther Connolly,' I said. Nothing smart-alec, or witty like a hero might say in a dime novel.

The guy shook his head. He reminded me of Mr Turner, the fat banker who'd stolen Ma and Pa's farm and any life I'd known out from under me.

'Well, Luther Connolly, whoever you are, you picked the wrong day to be here. We all did.'

He said that just as further rifle fire came from upstairs, and a blond man wearing more blood than can be good for anyone hurtled down the stairs with the lack of finesse only the dead can achieve.

'That crazy old black man's on his way,' the guy holding onto Mary-Ann shouted as he fumbled out of the way of the corpse rolling down the stairs.

The Turner lookalike took his eyes off me to the new danger, and I launched into him. He wasn't a tough guy at all. He was kind of feeble, not like a proper man at all, and clearly wasn't wise in the ways of fighting. Soon as I'd hit him and kept on pounding he was covering up in defence, thinking only to protect himself and not take a punch here and there so he could deliver a gunshot to me and finish me off. I went in on him all furious, hurling punches, angrier than ever.

'You dagarn coward,' I shouted as he rolled up on the floor covering himself. I kicked him a hard one, stamped on the hand holding the gun, hearing the bones break. He wailed like a girl. 'Get up and fight!!'

That he whimpered and rolled away to push back against the wall only made me the angrier. Here he was taking up a little girl and scaring her to death, wanting to do what Satan alone knew to her in the privacy of his own twisted soul, and the moment he had someone stand up to him he couldn't stomach a moment of it.

I was so concerned with beating on him that I plain forgot about the other man, the one holding Mary-Ann. It just clean passed from my head that he had a gun and might be brave enough to use it. I only realized he was there and could've killed me when my ears cleared from the ringing of one more rifle shot and I saw he was missing half of his head.

He toppled over, leaving Mary-Ann standing there, frightened and alone.

Clete had shot him from the top of the stairs.

Outside there was more shooting and then Jack Donovan shouted out, 'Now hold up here and let's finish this honourably.'

Clete came down the stairs, shot the guy I'd been beating on, and tossed me the rifle as he said, 'It's OK, I know how to handle this,' as he sank down and spoke softly to the girl. She looked

197

frozen into terror. 'Hey, there, Mary-Ann,' he said gently. 'It's all OK now.'

I caught the rifle and, crouching low, went over to the door. I peered out, and then without waiting for Clete, I stepped onto the walk.

16

I told you at the start of this document that this was the story of Smoke Winters, and how she fought and died in Inferno and then came back to fight again. Well, that's true. But it's also the story of Luther Connolly as well.

This is what I did. This is the part I played in the affair.

*   *   *

From out the door, I could see that a massacre had taken place on the street. Both horses were down, ripped and torn by bullets. One was half alive, which was a cruelty because it was never going to recover, and it kept nodding on its long neck, trying to find a way to stand. Wheat Rayne wasn't moving and I suspected if he could then he would, because he'd be drowning in that pool of blood in which he lay had he still been breathing. Danny was on the floor and had taken at least one bullet, but he had a rifle levelled now. I watched him click that trigger uselessly and slump sort of defeated, knowing he couldn't get to his horse and fumble around for more ammo.

When I looked to see who he was aiming at, there was Jack Donovan, strutting like a crow that had had its feathers ruffled and nothing more. He was out in the middle of the street, had a swagger to his walk.

I looked beyond him. Saw that the fat man Joad was twitching on the ground. Blood spurted from him in numerous places, like them blowholes you hear tell about. Spike, who couldn't make a sound with his mouth, now wasn't going to make any other kind of sound either. To add to the insult of losing his voice, he'd lost his face too. And while it had never been a pretty one, it was the only one he had. Both men were dead or well on the way to it. The gunhands who had come out to join in the shooting were sprawled motionless.

And Smoke . . .

Smoke was getting to her feet and sort of shambling out from behind the porch post she'd been using as cover. She moved out into the open. Her right arm hung uselessly, but in her left hand — her weaker hand for shooting, I'd always thought — she had Clete's big, boxy Colt. The one you had to really lever the hammer back on before you could pull the trigger.

Jack Donovan's jacket was torn up and his hat had either been shot from his head or tumbled to the ground at some point. But he must have a signed contract with the Devil, for it looked like not a single bullet had touched the flesh beneath his attire.

He said now, twirling his pistol, 'You come out here, little Cindy Winters, and I don't go over there and shoot your lasso hero. We finish this, you and I, on a quick draw.'

'I'm shooting left handed,' Smoke

told him. She was hoarse still, and breathless. Dust and gun smoke hung in the air, along with the iron scent of blood.

Donovan said, 'I'll allow you to hold it by your side. Cocked too. All you have to do is raise it quicker than I draw and pull the trigger. It's as fair a deal as you're gonna see today.'

Smoke thought on it and nodded and said, 'I accept that.'

'Let's do this, then.'

Smoke made an awkward job of pulling the trigger back on the Colt, to such a degree I hoped she was feigning it to make herself look weaker than she was. Then she let it hang to her side. Donovan holstered his pistol, grinned and walked down to meet Smoke.

They both came to a stop about twenty feet apart. Donovan was angled sideways on to me, from where I stood at the door. Smoke looked pained but I could see her concentration, reminding me of the first time I'd seen her, lining up her pine-cones and shooting them

202

so quickly they had splintered to a haze before I'd blinked.

'Well, I reckon this is it,' Donovan said. 'One of us wins, the other dies. Next time one of us blinks, we draw.'

No, I thought, looking at Smoke and seeing she hadn't been feigning her weakness: she really was done for. Not like this. It can't end like this.

I jumped off the boardwalk and shouted incoherently, swung Clete's rifle up, sighted along the barrel, and shot Donovan as he spun around to pull and sight on me. A plain and simple shot came from the rifle. The kickback whipped my shoulder hard. But the bullet whacked Donovan right in the middle of his head. I'd been aiming for his body, I'll be honest about that. But this worked better. His skull snapped back, and a gush of red and grey clutched at the air behind him and found nothing to hold onto, spattered to the ground, and Jack Donovan fell right over alongside it.

He didn't move. Didn't twitch. He

was done for. His gun had landed next to him.

Clete came out a moment later. Mary-Ann was holding his hand and hiding behind his thick legs. She looked frightened and lost, but there was a light in her eyes that I hadn't seen inside the building. There was life in them, and where there's life there's hope.

Smoke stood kind of dazed in the middle of the street. Danny shouted over to me, and I turned my head, about the only part of myself I could move right then, and looked at him. Next thing I knew, Clete was standing by me and his mouth was moving but I couldn't hear any words. Then Smoke was there, and she pulled the rifle out of my hands and was shouting at me, but I still didn't hear anything other than noise. I guess I was in a daze too.

★ ★ ★

We stood on the edge of town. It was high noon. Rain would come that evening but for now the place was dry as paper. We'd seen some of Inferno's residents, scuttling like shadows, moving out. A few had packs on their shoulders. None of them rode horses or carts. They went singly or in pairs. None of them looked healthy or like people you'd care to spend time with. They drifted out like tumbleweed.

Clete said, 'Don't be hard on the boy, he did right. Did what I'd have done.'

Smoke didn't say anything about that. She was sore that she hadn't had a chance to draw on Jack Donovan. She genuinely thought she could beat him with her weaker shooting hand.

Danny stood leaning on a stick. We'd torn off some strips of clothing to use as temporary bandages till we could get him to the doc. The bandages were already staining red.

'I was born here,' Smoke said flatly. 'It's no place for children. They shouldn't ever be brought here. Not after what the people here done to them.'

She looked at Mary-Ann. Then she lifted her head high, breathed in. She reached into a pocket, and with some discomfort extracted a set of lucifers.

'The place is like a tinderbox,' she said. 'But it's going to rain tonight. Best there's nothing here for the rain to save. You understand what I'm saying?'

We did, sort of. She handed out matchsticks to me. Clete was going to stay with Mary-Ann, who'd taken a liking to him, gather up some horses from what was passing for the livery at the end of one of the cross streets, and get us ready to move out and join the doc. Clete said there was a coach in there, polished to a high buff. One of the rich fat men's, I figured. Wheat was going to be cremated. He deserved better, but we were giving him all we had.

Not too long after, the fire had started, and it started quick and spread fast, which to my way of thinking meant it was something that was meant to be.

With the blaze roaring behind us, we left Inferno.

When we were all together again, as I sat in the back of Doc's buggy with Bobby Lee and Mary-Ann and we were heading back to Bradbury, I could still see the glow in the sky after sundown, reflecting off the gathering rain-clouds.

'After the fire cleanses things, the rain will wash it away,' Clete said, riding beside us with Danny, bandaged up, on a horse alongside him. Smoke sat up alongside Doc.

'That from the Bible?' I asked.

'Don't know. But it sounds like it should be.'

When the rain fell on the hot ashes and the beds of embers, all that remained of Inferno in other words, there'd be nothing but smoke curling in the air for a while. I imagined it would look like the horns of the Devil rising above hell itself.

I pointed that out to Smoke and I think she appreciated it.

Two months later Smoke left the jamboree show, lit out for places unknown. Bobby Lee brought up Mary-Ann as best he could, and from time to time when I was in the area I'd go a-calling and see how they were getting on. Mighty fine, was the answer. Danny merged his show with a bigger one and started playing large venues in cities, went over to Europe, touring through France and England with genuine Indians in his troupe as well. Clete lived for many years, eventually dying of old age. His one regret was that he never did see the girl he raised as his own again.

Me, I grew up, got wed, tried my hand back at farming, quit that and joined the Pinkerton National Detective Agency. Every now and again I'd hear rumours about this woman who helped children out. Word went that she rescued kidnapped boys and girls and hurt the men who'd been cruel to them. There was often no sign of the dens and pits in which the children had been hurt and these men festered. Often as not, they were raised to the ground by fire. Cleansed.

I once asked after a description of this woman. 'She's real quiet, speaks with a huskiness to her voice,' came the answer. 'You know she's serious, isn't to be messed with. But she's nice too. And beautiful, like an angel. She helped me. She shoots fast. And she's got the whitest hair I've ever seen. She's there and then she's gone, like smoke.'

Yeah, I thought on hearing this. Just like Smoke.